THE TRIUMPHANT
DAUGHTER

THE TRIUMPHANT DAUGHTER

UNSTOPPABLE LIV BEAUFONT™ BOOK 4

SARAH NOFFKE

MICHAEL ANDERLE

DISRUPTIVE IMAGINATION

LMBPN Publishing
PMB 196, 2540 South Maryland Pkwy
Las Vegas, NV 89109

First US Edition, March 2019

THE TRIUMPHANT DAUGHTER TEAM

Thanks to the JIT Readers

Jeff Goode
Crystal Wren
Misty Roa
James Caplan
John Ashmore
Larry Omans
Peter Manis
Kelly O'Donnell
Jeff Eaton
Micky Cocker
Angel LaVey

If I've missed anyone, please let me know!

Editor
The Skyhunter Editing Team

For Kathy.
Thank you for giving me my first fantasy book.
Since then, the world has been a better place.

CHAPTER ONE

The thick potion trickled from the corners of Wayne Grimson's lips as he gulped, holding the bottle with both hands. His arms were shaking.

"That's it," Adler Sinclair encouraged. "Just a bit more."

The lawyer did as he was told, drinking until the potion was nearly gone, only a small remnant clinging to the inside of the bottle.

His eyes were red and overflowing with tears when he lowered the bottle to his polished desk.

"Now remember, you aren't to ever disclose who you work for," Adler began, speaking the enchantment as he'd done so many other times to the lawyer. The potion wore off every few weeks, but it was worth redosing him. Wayne Grimson had proven to be reliable, doing Adler's bidding and keeping attention off him.

"The threat of torture and death will not break my bonds," Wayne said in a robotic voice. "No matter what, I will not speak."

Adler nodded. "And you can't be controlled by any other. No one but me can force anything upon you."

Wayne wiped the sides of his mouth, straightening and starting to look more like his old self, although that part of him had probably been lost for a long time. He wouldn't truly remember who he was ever again. That was the price of the molding potion, and to Adler Sinclair, it was absolutely worth it.

Mortals were expendable. Some didn't see it that way, but they also didn't understand the full scope of things—that if it weren't for him and his ancestors and what they'd done, magic would have been lost long ago.

"I answer to only you," Wayne said, blinking and looking around the office like he'd suddenly remembered where he was.

Adler ran his finger over the blade of the sword sitting across the front of the desk, marveling at its craftsmanship —the one that Wayne had recovered. Adler may have had no tolerance for the savage giants, but he could appreciate the work they did. For a long time, he'd tried to obtain a giant-forged sword but had failed. There were just not that many in the world, and the ones that were, the giants protected on the scarce bit of land where they'd been "assigned" to live. But a personal weapon didn't matter as much as having secured the one before him. This one held memories and things that no others should know about. That was why it had been locked up in the National History Museum for the better part of a century.

Until Liv Beaufont ruined everything.

Adler reminded himself that she was just a dumb girl. At first, he'd worried that she had unprecedented powers or was going to be a problem like her parents and siblings had been. Her power level was higher than most...well, anyone's, but he was sure it would normalize in time. He'd concluded she just kept showing up in the wrong places at the wrong times. Dumb luck. The demon-hunting case was perfect for her. It would either take her out or humble her —he didn't care which one.

"I want you to continue to have your people keep an eye on Ms. Beaufont," Adler ordered Wayne.

The lawyer nodded mechanically.

Adler had thought that forcing Liv to move into the House of Seven was the best way to keep tabs on her. However, he needed the sword back, and the leverage he had on her was enough to get her to release it. After deliberation, he realized that the inexperienced warrior would be more trouble for him living at the House. It was better if she simply risked her life slaying demons daily and stayed out of the House as much as possible.

Running his hands over the giant's sword again, Adler muttered a series of incantations, glamouring the object so that it appeared to be an oversized poster in a cardboard, circular case. It was still heavy as hell when he picked it up, carrying it over his shoulder. He'd thought that hiding the weapon in plain sight was the best way to keep it away from the giants, who would feel the history pulsing within it and remember the past. He wouldn't be making that mistake again. Turbinger would disappear, never to be seen again. There were places that only he knew about where things could be hidden, especially within the House of Seven.

Adler had always been a fan of hiding things in plain

sight because most didn't even know where to look. Most were so inundated with the thoughts in their heads or their own selfish desires that they didn't see what was right in front of them. And even if they did, the enchantments in the House were strong enough to make them forget. That was why no one remembered the Black Void between the Chamber of the Tree and the residential corridor in the House of Seven. Even if anyone saw it, they wouldn't know how to enter, and better yet, they'd be terrified to do so.

The sword would go in there and be safe for the rest of time. Adler was looking forward to reassuring the God Magician that things were back on track. First, though, he'd have to wake him. That filled him with both anticipation and trepidation. Things were always unpredictable when the God Magician stirred, his power being both great and diabolical. Adler couldn't control everything when the God Magician was awake. He'd been working on that, though. He believed in maintaining the balance. That was why he'd risked everything to keep what his ancestors had started a secret, and he believed that this responsibility extended to all areas of the House of Seven.

Yes, he'd wake the God Magician on schedule. Thankfully, it would take the deity some time to recover, giving Adler a chance to avoid the complications that had happened last time, creating suspicion.

He let out a reassuring breath and reminded himself that things were different now. The House was different. He had selected the Councilors and warriors who made it up, lemmings and simple soldiers who did as they were told, not seeing that which he wanted to keep hidden.

CHAPTER TWO

The snow crunched under Liv Beaufont's boot, and it sank in several inches. She took another step, feeling like the blanket of seemingly endless snow might blind her soon.

Stefan had told her to stay put, hiding behind the embankment until she heard his signal. Glancing down at Plato, Liv grimaced.

"Why Wyoming and other horribly freezing places? Why can't demons hide in Cabo San Lucas next to a pool with a cabana?" she mused, pulling her fur-lined cape around her tighter as she shivered.

Plato, who didn't seem the least bit bothered by the freezing temperature, gave her a sympathetic look. "I thought this was an improvement over northern Alaska."

"It's not," Liv replied. "Damn it, no more demon hunting in icy climates. If they want to prowl Earth, then they need to choose places more like hell. Wait, is that why they go to icy places? Is this the real hell?"

"I think they come for the mortals rather than the temperatures," Plato explained, sniffing the air.

"Are people in colder climates easier to corrupt, do you think?" Liv asked.

"I think it depends on the demon, which depends on who they were when they were alive," Plato related. "Some want to corrupt the innocent, spreading evil. Some like to perpetuate that which is already corrupt."

"How do you know this? Never mind. You're not going to tell me, and I'd rather you keep your air of mystery."

Plato's ears perked up slightly. "I might in this instance have been willing to tell you how I know that information."

"Oh, really?" Liv inquired, holding Bellator, her sword, firmly in both hands.

"No, not really," Plato replied slyly.

Liv pursed her lips. "You're such a tease."

"Speaking of teases." Plato lifted his chin, directing his gaze over his shoulder. "It looks like the bait worked."

Liv smiled with delight. "Which means it's go time." Even though she could hear the noises Plato was referring to, she waited for the signal. Timing was everything, as Stefan and she had discussed, reviewing the strategy time and time again.

The mehhhing of the scared goat would have made Liv's heart constrict with guilt, but she reminded herself that it wasn't a real goat. It was merely an apparition that Stefan had created as bait.

The goat jumped over Liv's and Plato's heads. They were tucked up against the embankment, which dropped off several feet. The goat didn't stop after landing awkwardly in the snow, just kept scurrying down the steep hillside, its hooves sliding as it cried out in wild desperation.

A low whistle pierced the air, making Liv tense. That was it—the signal. She readied Bellator, noticing that Plato had disappeared.

The first demon soared over her head, clawing through the air, legs pedaling like he was riding an invisible bike. He landed with a crunch in the untouched snow, his hands down and his focus on the goat, which was quickly getting away. The beast, an exceptionally ugly creature with red scales over its head and neck and a forked tongue, growled.

"Hey, Baldy, why don't you pick on someone your own size?" Liv called to the monster, getting his attention at once.

He spun to her, a vicious snarl ripping from his mouth. The demon was taller and broader than her, and fast. However, she was prepared, swinging Bellator at him as he sprang in her direction. The blade cut across his chest, spraying black blood over the white snow.

"Oh, hell, I was going to make a snowman out of that snow," Liv grumbled as the beast grabbed his chest, writhing in pain from being marked with Bellator. "You ruined everything with your blood. Oh, and also by being a nasty demon."

Liv was just about to swing Bellator again and finish the monster off when another demon soared overhead, landing close to the first. This new one spun, catching sight of Liv immediately. *So, apparently the goat race was over,* she thought, her eyes darting between the two.

The unharmed second demon lunged at Liv, screeching horribly. She thrust her foot at him, trying to push him back. Instead, he grabbed her foot, twisting it to the right and forcing Liv off her feet. Her face met the snow, which pierced her skin with cold.

Before the beast could jump on her back, Liv rolled to the side, then popped to her feet. She'd dropped the sword during the fall, and it was now partially covered in snow.

Liv lifted her hand and directed it at the uninjured demon, hitting him in the chest with a gale-force wind. He flew back several yards, giving her a moment to scramble for Bellator and recover it. The injured demon lumbered in her direction, but she wasn't worried about him. He was on the decline, albeit slowly. The second one would be easy enough to take down once she finished off the first. Bellator made demon hunting a breeze since the blade was lethal to the demons. She started regretting the bout of confidence when a third demon launched himself over the embankment, landing with a thud that shook the ground under her feet.

This one was massive.

"Well, looks like the party officially started," Liv said, backing up as the meaty beast squared his shoulders and regarded her with the deep-seated hatred demons felt for all humans.

"Thing is, I didn't bring party favors for you all, so someone is going to get their feelings hurt."

The three demons had her cornered and moved in slowly with their shoulders down and teeth bared. The smell was overwhelming. Liv sucked in a breath through her mouth and remembered her training.

We are one, she thought, gripping Bellator tightly, and something shifted in her. She wasn't a Warrior holding a sword. She *was* the sword, and the sword was her. They were one, moving together like the way a rush of droplets of water barrels over a waterfall. Separate and yet together. Soft and unyielding.

As the demons broke formation, Liv brought Bellator around and overhead, not even knowing what she was going to do. The blade ripped across two of the demons, knocking them back. She hiked up her leg, back-kicking the first demon and sending him into a pile of freshly-packed snow.

The other two were already on their feet, although they weren't quiet about their injuries. Bellator's mark would eventually kill them, but for now, it only slowed them down. As they barreled in her direction, Liv held Bellator above her head and threw it like a spear at the smaller of the two demons, impaling his chest. He stumbled back, clutching the blade as unintelligible language spewed over his blackened lips.

Weaponless, and with the larger demon lumbering in her direction, Liv waited until he was almost upon her. Then she moved the way Akio had taught her—with blinding momentum, blurring as she sprinted across the snow, away from the beast's clutches. She knew that the trick would draw down her magical reserves, but it would be worth it if things went according to plan. Fighting three at the same time was *not* the plan, but then nothing ever went to plan when it came to battling demons.

The beast realized too late that Liv had swerved around him and nearly slammed into the side of the embankment. Had he done so, it would have saved her the trouble, but she didn't mind. Holding up her hand, she muttered a single incantation. The ground rumbled under their feet, and the mountain of snow crumbled over the cliff's edge, burying the demon.

Liv backed up, trying to stay out of the mini-avalanche she'd caused. For some reason, this reminded her of her parents' death. She hadn't been there when they supposedly fell from the Matterhorn, but she had dreamed about it often, seeing her parents battling snowstorms and trying to help each other survive until something took them both down to the bottom—a fall neither survived.

The snarling of the beasts behind her brought her back to the present moment. The sight of the demon clawing at Bellator, which was protruding from its chest, was creepy and strange. Liv shook her head, realizing it was time to end this.

She strode over to the deadly demon she'd once have feared. However, she had found that there were worse things than evil dressed as a monster. No, worse was disguised evil. Buried secrets. A mystery linked to forgotten history. At least with a demon, she knew what she was getting every time, and she felt no remorse for ridding the Earth of them. If anything, she felt like she was saving a lost soul. And in truth, that was exactly what a demon hunter did. They did it the right way when they could.

Liv grabbed the hilt of the sword, enjoying the moment that her hand met the metal and she reconnected with her other half. With a yank, she released Bellator from the demon's chest cavity, black blood spurting all over the white snow.

"*Metuendas Dcemonis violentias,*" Liv began, repeating the

ancient words that would release the soul trapped inside the demon. Simultaneously she swung Bellator over her head, using that momentum to stab the demon who thought he was about to sneak up on her. It was an injury most demons could survive, but not when done with Bellator. Liv twisted the sword, watching as the demon coughed up blood.

She pulled up her foot and kicked the demon off her sword, allowing it to lead the way. *"Dimittere unam animam de amicae tuae involasti, permittens eos tandem requiem,"* she continued. To her surprise, the sword came straight up in and in an arch like she was a batter hitting a grand slam. It sliced across the demon at her back, cutting off a portion of its top half. Liv didn't have a chance to determine what portion of the top half. Two down. One to go.

Under the fallen snow, the last demon was stirring at last, his screeching growing louder.

Liv positioned herself just in front of him, gripping the bloody blade with burning heat in her eyes. She pulled in a breath. *"Ad infernum, a quo factum est tibi in sempiternum in ipse comburetis,"* she nearly yelled as the demon shot out of the snow. Before it was even close to out all the way, Liv swung Bellator around, lopping off its head, leaving her in silence. She looked around at the evidence of the massacre marking the snow before peering at one of her most trusted companions—Bellator.

CHAPTER THREE

"So you didn't need my help?" Stefan said. He was standing majestically at the top of the snow embankment holding a sword and breathing heavily, his brow covered in sweat.

Liv gazed at the severed head of the biggest demon lying on the snow and shrugged. "Yeah, I guess not." She motioned to the blanket of black-stained snow. "If you want to clean up, though, that would be welcome."

He laughed, his voice echoing over the hills. "Oh, no. I'm not cleaning up after your blood bath. Getting demon blood out of clothing is the worst."

Liv tried to laugh, but it was fake. Even though Stefan was acting strong, she saw the fatigue etching his features. Every day it was deeper, making him look darker—taking away from his human features. Each day he looked less like himself, and they ignored it; pretended it wasn't happening to him...to them. That things weren't a day, a week, or a month from changing.

One day, she might be hunting *him*.

The ache of that potential reality was too much for her to process, so she pressed it down and pretended that he'd always breathed heavily and had the pale complexion and hollow eyes. In the back of her mind, she remembered Stefan Ludwig as he had been before the demon bite got worse. She remembered him as being strong and outrunning her. Liv remembered him as agile, chopping down the wood for the fires at night. Now, he wasn't capable of even gathering water before dinner, his chest heaving dramatically from the simple act of breathing.

Presently though, he was trying to pretend he was strong and she could have used his help. Liv indulged him with a smile.

"Was that all of them?" Liv asked.

Stefan gazed around at the snowy hillside. "Yeah, that's it."

That was what Stefan was good at. They'd actually made the perfect team because the demon blood in him enabled him to find and track them. He knew where they needed to go, saving weeks of time. Never had they found Sabatore. No, finding the demon who had bitten Stefan was not part of the equation. However, they slaughtered many others. Well, Liv did. Stefan led them to the right location, and Liv used Bellator to make the job easy. It was a great arrangement, except that it was getting harder.

Stefan could point her in the right direction, but then he preferred to stay back. It was getting harder for him to slaughter demons since he saw them as his own. He recounted to Liv over the evening fires that he felt more akin to them than magicians these days. She shook her head, refilling his water, telling him they'd find Sabatore and save him. However, she didn't believe that anymore. What they needed was a strategy they hadn't tried before. Tracking down demons and questioning them wasn't working any longer. They needed to revamp things and do something unconventional. Stefan didn't have much more time and they both knew it, even if no one said it out loud.

"We're no closer to finding Sabatore," Liv finally said after a moment, suddenly feeling the cold after the intense battle.

"Well, then we start again tomorrow," Stefan stated, sniffing the air. "There are more demons to the east."

Liv shook her head. "No, I think we need better eyes." Sensing Stefan's reluctance, she corrected herself. "I mean, we need to use our contacts. You yourself said that you were blocked from him, so finding him ourselves won't work. We need an expert on the subject. Someone who watches such activity."

"What do you have in mind, Beaufont?" Stefan asked, climbing down a safe area of the embankment and taking the spot next to her.

"Well, I've used the brownies before for such things," Liv began. "They have eyes everywhere. Maybe they can help us. I have a friend in the government center."

"Of course you do," Stefan said with a laugh, which made him cough, spitting up blood. They both pretended like that hadn't happened as Liv kicked at the snow.

"Yeah, I'm now thinking that maybe they know where Sabatore is," Liv continued in a hurry, trying to cover her nervousness. She knew all too well that Stefan could turn into a demon at any moment. No longer did she worry about herself if she was caught in that situation. She slept with Bellator beside her, and anyway, she hardly slept. She worried about Stefan. If...*when* he turned, she had orders that she wouldn't ignore. And killing what Stefan Ludwig became? That would forever live in her soul. Still, that was the agreement they'd come to after many late-night discussions. She'd made promises, though. She'd stand by them. And she believed in them. She just hoped things didn't come to that.

"Okay, fine," Stefan agreed, his voice tired. "You enlist your brownies. But you'll have to do that after you update the council."

Liv looked up at him suddenly. "We're hunting demons, as they requested. Why do we need to give them an update?"

Stefan shook his head, looking away from the scene of the slaughter, unable to stomach it. "It's easier if you check in with them regularly; better that way. Adler gets unruly if you let too much time go by."

"Well, why do *I* have to do the update?" Liv asked, but they both knew the answer.

Stefan was in no shape to go before the council. They'd know immediately that there was something wrong with him. They had to buy a little more time. Keep the council from getting suspicious. Find a different strategy. All they needed was time—and a miracle wouldn't hurt.

"Yeah, fine," Liv said. "I'll cover for your ass. But this is the last time."

He winked at her, hiding his wheezing breath. "Thanks. Last time, I promise."

CHAPTER FOUR

E ven though Liv knew she was close to being late for
the meeting with the Seven, she couldn't force
herself to look away from the Black Void.

"Black Void," she muttered to herself. Why did that
sound so right? She hadn't known what to call the swirling
darkness before. No one knew what it was, so they hadn't
called it anything. Hell, most didn't even notice it when she
pointed it out. They'd see it and then forget it immediately.

Liv didn't understand. How could magicians walk by
the black abyss all the time, but no one saw it? Her parents
had always dismissed her when she cringed as they walked
by it on the way to the residential wing, telling her it was
nothing. It didn't *feel* like nothing. It felt like a foreboding
presence that might squash her if she got near it.

Actually, it felt like the very end of the Earth, and more
than once she had the urge to hurl herself over it. That had
been after her parents' death, though, when Liv had feared
she had lost all hope for any happiness in the future. With
her world destroyed and her heart broken by the commu-

17

nity she was supposed to trust, Liv had sunk to her lowest, having many deranged impulses. But that was one of the many reasons she left the House of Seven—wishing to be a mortal living in a less complicated world.

The Black Void was different now, but Liv didn't know how or why. She couldn't look away from it easily. Although it was only darkness, she could have sworn she saw a rotating pattern drawing her in, begging her to continue staring. And then she heard it!

A ghostly whisper emerged from the Black Void, and Liv leaned closer. What was it chanting? Was that her name? No, but whatever it was, it sent a shiver down her spine. It seemed almost like a threat. Liv strained to hear it, nearly hanging over the edge into the Black Void.

"Back away or else," she thought she heard a voice say. That couldn't be right. Liv pressed her eyes shut, focusing on nothing but those four words as they were repeated, trying to discern them.

"Ms. Beaufont!"

Liv's eyes popped open, and she straightened to face Decar Sinclair. His long white hair was braided down his back today, contrasting with his black robes. Disapproval was heavy in his light-colored eyes, spraying the area around them with wrinkles. "What are you doing?"

Liv kept herself from looking back at the Black Void. Something told her she shouldn't ask Decar if he saw it too or knew what it was.

"I'm looking for Clark," she lied. "We're playing a game of hide and seek, and I thought he might be disguised as the wall here." She pointed to the area beside the Door of Reflection.

Decar shook his head. "You and your brother play such games? Don't you have more pressing matters?"

Liv couldn't tell him that it was her brilliant little sister she played this game with and that she was incredible with disguises, so she simply nodded. "Yep, it's our thing."

"Don't you think you're both too old for such things?" Decar asked, condescension heavy in his tone.

Good, he believes I'm an immature brat now, Liv thought, grateful she'd thrown him off, even if it made her look ridiculous.

"I'm sort of having a second childhood," she explained with no shame on her face.

"Well, if you can act like an adult for a little while, the meeting is about to start." Decar strode past her and straight through the Door of Reflection, disappearing at once.

"I'd rather act like a kid than a stuffy old magician who is zero fun at all," Liv muttered to herself, looking over her shoulder at the Black Void before heading for the Door of Reflection. She didn't know what it was, or if it was hiding something, or if she had in fact heard a threat from it, but she was determined to find out more.

What blanketed her vision next was a blow to the stomach. Before her, she saw her parents standing together, their arms crossed, shaking their heads in disappointment. "You really let us down, Olivia," her father said, his blue eyes brimming with frustration.

Liv's mother dropped her chin as if she couldn't stand to look at her. "We were counting on you."

Tears welled in her eyes, threatening to burst from her, and Liv's insides were shaking. She hadn't felt this close to losing it...well, since after her parent's death. Pushing down the ache, she reminded herself that this wasn't real. These were her fears appearing as waking dreams. It might feel very real, but it wasn't. It might appear like she could reach out and touch her parents, but they weren't there. It was all her imagination.

Stepping through the Door of Reflection, Liv sped toward her spot, keeping her head down to cover any rogue emotions she hadn't corralled yet. She nearly walked into the white tiger, who was standing on her spot, staring casually at the council.

Liv halted abruptly, hoping that the tiger would realize he was in her place and move. She even considered that he'd glance at her with those old-soul eyes and then move. Instead, he stoically stared ahead, not seeming to notice her.

Adler, as usual, was lecturing Trudy about something. The Warrior had dropped her head with a look that was undoubtedly shame.

Since no one had seemed to notice Liv yet, she cleared her throat quietly, hoping to gain the white tiger's attention. It didn't work.

"How many times have we been through this?" Adler asked, borrowing his brother's condescending tone. "Unregistered magicians aren't given second chances. If you let them go, they aren't going to immediately run off and register with the House. They are rebels who are going to revel in the fact that they've beaten the system yet again. You realize you've made us look like fools, don't you?"

"It's just that it was a family," Trudy explained, her tone

troubled. "The parents had young children, and it didn't seem right—"

"The law is clear on how we are to handle offenders, regardless of whether they have offspring," Adler interrupted.

"Actually, we should be even more strict on offenders who have children, since they are going to perpetuate the problem by handing down their rebellious ways to their offspring," Bianca imparted.

Lorenzo nodded, stroking his black goatee. "That's a valid point."

"Justice is about doing the right thing," Liv found herself spouting before she could stop. "Just because something is the law doesn't make it the correct action to take."

Clark pressed his fist into his forehead.

How come he didn't realize by now that I was going to open my mouth and say something that would make him cringe? she wondered. *That was her role. He was the uptight rule follower, and she was the rebel. That was part of the balance, right?*

Adler directed his cold eyes at Liv. "Ms. Beaufont, why haven't you taken your spot?"

Liv pointed at the tiger, who still didn't seem to notice her standing there.

Hester and Raina snickered, finding this amusing.

"Ms. Beaufont, we don't have time for your games," Adler said, not finding this entertaining. "Take your spot, and we'll hear your update on the demon case."

Liv cleared her throat loudly, looking intently at the white tiger. He didn't move. What was she supposed to do, push him out of the way? The only time she'd dared to pet the tiger, the council had nearly fallen over in surprise.

Feeling lost, Liv threw up her hands. "I'm not sure how I'm supposed to take my spot when the tiger is occupying it."

Haro lifted an eyebrow, his lips pursed. "She's correct."

Adler jerked his head to the side, giving the tiger a serious expression. "Move on, then. A Warrior can't address the council unless they're in position."

The tiger blinked up at him impassively.

"If the white tiger isn't moving, maybe that's a message," Haro mused.

Alder shot him a frustrated look. "Nothing that animal does makes sense. How is this a message?"

"It may not make sense to you," Raina began, "but the role of the white tiger and black crow is to create balance."

"I know that," Adler nearly yelled.

"Maybe," Haro began, thinking, "the tiger is trying to say that Warrior Beaufont shouldn't be here today."

Adler sighed. "I think we put too much stock in the strange and mysterious things that animal does. I for one think we should start ignoring it."

This brought startled reactions from many of the council members.

"The Founders stated that the tiger and crow were always supposed to be part of these proceedings," Haro stated. "It was mine and the Beaufonts' grandfathers who supposedly created the animals to ensure—"

"Yes, I know that," Adler cut in. "Yes, yes, it's all about balance. But how are we supposed to conduct business with the tiger interfering?"

"I can just stand there," Liv said, gesturing to the spot beside the tiger.

"Fine," Adler said dismissively. "Report to the council about your case."

"We've been killing lots of demons," Liv began proudly.

Adler's eyelids fluttered with annoyance. "Yes, we know that, Ms. Beaufont. Do you want to be more specific?"

"The nest in the north has almost been wiped out," Liv stated.

"That's most impressive," Hester exclaimed, her eyes darting to Stefan's spot. "And where is Warrior Ludwig?"

Hester was the only person besides Liv who knew Stefan was battling a demon bite. As a healer, she'd know he had limited time. "He is tracking more demons in the territory. I came to deliver the report."

"Very well, then," Adler said, looking bored. "And Decar, you're done with your case?"

His brother nodded, his chin held high.

Usually that was Liv's cue to leave, but given the strange business with the white tiger and extra activity of the other Council members, she decided to stick around.

"Good, good," Adler said, offering the first bit of praise Liv had ever heard from him. "It's that time of the century again. We need you to pay the giants a visit on the Isle of Man."

Liv's mouth slammed shut as she froze, listening intently. That was where Rory's mother had taken Turbinger. It was apparently where most of the giants lived, away from society and other magical creatures.

"Yes. Although we're certain that the giants will decline to join the treaty," Bianca stated, "it states that we are to offer them a chance every one hundred years."

"You, Decar, are to go to the Isle of Man and explain to

them the benefits of being part of the alliance," Adler said. "They will say no, and we'll have fulfilled our mandate for another century."

"I'll do it," Liv nearly shouted.

All eyes swiveled to her.

Liv swallowed. "I just meant that I've never been to the Isle of Man, and I'm really fascinated by the giant culture."

Clark's eyes looked close to popping out of his skull.

"I mean, since I've never been around giants," Liv continued, "I was thinking this would be a good opportunity to test my diplomacy skills."

"Ms. Beaufont," Adler began in a tired voice, "you already have a case."

"Yeah, but I can do both," Liv replied at once. "I need a break from fighting demons nonstop, and maybe I can clear any that are on the island."

Bianca rolled her eyes. "There are no demons on the island. The giants ensure that."

"Well, there's another great reason for me to go," Liv stated. "I might be able to learn what demon repellant they use to keep the beasts off their turf."

All Liv knew for sure was that Decar couldn't go to the giants' island where Turbinger was located. He might sense the weapon, or find out that they'd made a replica.

Adler paused, seeming to consider this.

"We have spoken before about Warrior Beaufont's negotiation skills and how good they are," Hester offered.

Bianca laughed, a high-pitched shrill sound. "We all know this is just a show for the giants' sake. They aren't going to entertain our offer, and they aren't even civilized enough to negotiate with."

Raina seemed to be restraining herself. "Although I don't think that's true, it is our duty to try to include the giants. Liv had luck with the fae, and she might be the right person for this case as well."

Adler sighed. "Fine, if you really want it, Ms. Beaufont. But know that this doesn't relieve you from your current case. You'll be expected to do both."

"That's perfect," Liv said at once. "I hate sleeping."

Before Liv was done speaking, Adler turned his attention back to his brother. "Decar, since Ms. DeVries has so much trouble bringing down unregistered magicians, why don't you take over controlling those delinquents?"

Decar nodded at once. "Yes, that won't be a problem."

Damn it, Liv thought. She's gotten the giants' case but lost the unregistered magicians' one. She knew that Trudy had been doing the right thing. Not only was it immoral to "dispose" of unregistered magicians who had young children, but it was wrong to impose such strict regulations on their community in the first place. She sensed that more people than just Trudy DeVries agreed with that. When she wasn't hunting demons and negotiating with giants, she was going to have to figure out how to bring justice to that part of the House of Seven. Regulations and controls were one thing. Blindly punishing law-breakers was another.

CHAPTER FIVE

"I just don't think it's a good idea," Liv said, tossing the red ball back to Sophia. Her little sister was sitting cross-legged on the carpet in her and Clark's residence, the stuffed animals that she'd enchanted marching in a parade at her back.

Sophia caught the ball, huffing. "Please."

"That's not how it works, Soph," Liv stated. "You don't just beg and get your way."

"How am I supposed to know how anything works?" the little eight-year-old argued.

Liv indicated the menagerie of stuffed animals, who were performing a pretty impressive choreographed dance. "I think you do all right figuring things out on your own. If the council or anyone knew that you already had your magic and it was extraordinary, they wouldn't let you leave the House until you were my age."

"They'd lock my magic," Sophia said with a huge frown, tossing the ball back to Liv.

"I want to help you, but honestly, I've got to figure out

this business that Rory learned from Turbinger," Liv said, off in thought.

"You said he hasn't figured it all out yet, right?" Sophia asked.

Liv nodded. "Yeah, all he knows so far is that there was a massive war between magicians and mortals. He can't pinpoint the timeline or anything else that will shine any more light on the mystery."

"I'm really great at being a detective," Sophia offered.

Liv rolled her eyes at her little sister. "That's not going to work."

"Didn't you say that Rory has kittens?"

"Yeah, he's got a litter birthed at some point," Liv joked.

"I've never seen a kitten," Sophia countered.

"Soph!" Liv warned.

"Or a sunset," she went on.

"I can't. Clark would kill me."

"And I hear the ocean smells salty. Is that true?" Sophia asked, batting her eyelashes.

Liv pressed her eyes closed, unsure of what to do. When she opened them, she couldn't bear the look on her little sister's face. If she'd ever had any strength to withstand her persuasion, it was gone when she looked into those beautiful blue eyes.

She sighed, resigned. "Yeah, fine. Put on your shoes."

"You shouldn't have brought her here," Rory complained. He was sitting in his oversized chair and watching as the kittens crawled over Sophia, making the young girl giggle.

"She's never played with kittens," Liv argued. "I had to. The poor girl has been around tiny dragons and pixies, but she's had no exposure to mortal things."

"There's a reason that she's been locked up at the House of Seven," Rory stated. "Young magicians are unpredictable. It's unclear exactly when they'll get their magic, and having them around electrical devices can be risky."

"Well, Sophia already has her magic," Liv countered.

"I know," Rory said with a heavy sigh. "I can feel it. She definitely is taking after you."

Liv was surprised by this. "Me? You mean, you don't think my magic will normalize? The council keeps telling me it will."

Rory shook his head. "This *is* your normal. If anything, I think your magic will get stronger."

"Whoa," Liv breathed. "And don't worry, Sophia only came here. We learned our lesson when she set off all the devices in John's store during the party."

Sophia giggled as Junebug attacked her patent leather shoes, playfully biting at her toes.

Because the sour expression hadn't disappeared from Rory's face, Liv continued, "Our parents believed in us going out of the House and exploring. They made our education organic, taking us on adventures. If they were here and raising Sophia, she wouldn't be confined. They never agreed with the guideline put down by the House."

Rory softened, but only slightly. "Fine. I get it, and I don't agree either with sheltering children. I get why well-meaning magical races do it with their own, but I don't like it. I wasn't allowed to leave the island until I was of age, and it's why I don't want to go back."

Liv took a seat on the lumpy couch, her eyes darting to where Turbinger used to hang over the fireplace. "Speaking of the Isle of Man, I volunteered for a case."

Howls of laughter spilled from Rory's mouth when Liv told him about the case with the giants, scaring three of the kittens and making them dart under the sofa. "You should have let Decar take the case."

"What? I couldn't do that," Liv argued. "He might find out about Turbinger. And why are you laughing?"

Rory paused, admiration on his face. "That's true about Turbinger. Decar would have, and then it would have all been over. We'd possibly have another war on our hands. However, you traded your life to keep that sword protected and secret."

Sophia looked up, her blue eyes wide.

Liv waved off her concern. "Don't mind Rory. He loves to exaggerate. You should hear some of the tall tales he tries to pass off as true."

"Ha-ha," Rory said with no inflection. "And I'm not exaggerating. Those giants will have you roasting over a fire for supper minutes after you set foot on the island."

"And here I've been trying to convince the others that giants are civilized creatures," Liv stated.

"We are, in our own way," Rory explained. "However, the original tribe has no tolerance for magicians, especially ones who trespass on their land. There are still bitter feelings over how things have been handled in the past. The agreement was that the giants would mostly confine themselves to the Isle of Man, and in return, we wouldn't have to deal with the House's regulations."

"But *you* don't live there. And I've seen other giants, like that one time at that bar with the gnomes."

Rory nodded. "Yes, but we live in secret for the most part. Even if the council finds out about us, they don't mind as long as we keep to ourselves, but they don't want a few thousand giants trying to live among society. And honestly, the giants prefer to live away from the rest, who they see as wasteful and superficial."

"Well, I don't see what the difference is between Decar going there or me," Liv stated.

"The difference is that Decar is a magician who has displayed his power by killing many giants," Rory explained. "The giants may hate him for it, but he played things right, showing his dominance. I wager that he could step onto that island, invite the chief to participate in the alliance and then take his written refusal back to the council completely unscathed. You? Well, they will see you as fresh meat."

"Damn it." Liv sighed. "This is the kingdom of the Fae all over again."

Rory nodded. "And unfortunately for you, there is no fancy outfit you can wear or gift you can offer the giants to ease their tensions."

Sophia looked up suddenly, her eyes bright. "I think you're wrong. There is an outfit that could work. What if Liv showed up looking like Decar?"

Rory's mouth opened like he was going to say something, but he just shook his head.

"Soph, do you think you can pull off a disguising spell like that?" Liv asked.

Sophia thought for a moment, combing her hands over

the backs of the kittens crawling over her lap. "I don't know. I've never tried anything like that, but I don't see why not."

Rory stood, towering over them. "That's really complicated magic. And if it wears off while you're on the island, you might as well slit your throat before the giants do."

"Sophia is the best at doing disguises," Liv argued. "If anyone can do it, it's her."

The little magician blushed. "Thank you. But also, shouldn't the giants like Liv because she recovered Turbinger for them?"

"Great point!" Liv exclaimed, hope blossoming in her chest.

Rory regarded Sophia with a thoughtful expression, then knelt beside her, one of his knees popping loudly. "Yes, that *would* have helped Liv's chances, but no one knows that Turbinger is back in the giants' hands. My mum thought it best not to tell anyone yet. She fears there will be a fight over it once word gets out, and she's trying to decide how best to handle it."

"So the best option is to have me disguise her as Decar, a magician they fear?" Sophia asked, sounding much too old for her age.

Rory still looked skeptical.

"If Sophia can pull off the spell, which I believe she can," Liv began, "then would that work?"

Rory picked up Junebug, stopping him from attacking Sophia's foot any longer, and held the kitten to his chest as if enjoying the warmth. "It could work, but you have to approach the chief and discuss things as Decar would. If anything is off, they will grow suspicious."

"So, you mean I have to be a giant asshole?" Liv asked.

Rory glanced over his shoulder at her, grimacing. "Language," he scolded.

"Sorry, of course," Liv stated. "I didn't mean to use the word giant in such a way."

He shook his head. "That's not what I meant."

"I'll need some time to work on the spell," Sophia said with a giggle, watching Rory cuddle the tiny kitten.

"That's fine," Liv stated. "I've got demons to hunt down."

"Okay, this might work," Rory concluded, appearing less stressed about the idea than before. "If you play it right, the chief will decline your offer of alliance, giving you the formal reply that you can take back to the House of Seven. Mission accomplished."

Liv smiled, grateful that the plan had come together. "And they'll conclude that the giants are still barbarians and leave them alone for another century, keeping Turbinger safe."

"What are you going to do with the kittens when they are big enough?" Sophia asked, the smile on her face wide as Samson played with the sash on her dress. "Can I have one if I can hide it in our residence at the House?"

"Rory is going to eat them," Liv said before he could answer.

Again, he gave her a punishing look turning his attention to Sophia. "I'm going to be finding them homes soon, but I don't think that it would be good for you to keep one. It will draw suspicion if anyone wonders where you got it."

Sophia nodded, understanding. "I figured. No one at the House of Seven has an ordinary pet like a housecat."

"That's true," Rory said, something sparking in his eyes. "However, I may be able to find you a special magical creature that you could have at the House. Something that would make more sense for a magician to have."

Sophia's eyes brightened with excitement. "Really? Thank you! That would be wonderful."

Liv smiled in appreciation. "And hey, I'm a magician, and I have a cat."

Rory shook his head. "We both know Plato is anything but ordinary."

CHAPTER SIX

The chilly London air wrapped around Liv as she stepped through the portal onto Roya Lane. She pulled her cape tighter, keeping the hood over her head. The last time she was at Government Center, she'd received many speculative glances from other magical creatures, and she was hoping to avoid that this time.

"And there is my sixty-fifth favorite person," Rudolf said, appearing beside her seemingly out of nowhere.

Liv offered him her best annoyed glare. "'Sixty-fifth?' Wow, thanks. You don't even make the top one hundred on *my* list."

"Yes, I do," he teased, looking her over. "I liked you better in that tight green number. Why don't you go back to that?"

"Because my job is to kick ass for a living, which is tough to do with a spandex dress riding up."

"There was once a fae warrior who used her provocative skills to distract her enemy, thereby winning the advantage and ending them," Rudolf imparted.

"What happened to this fae?" Liv asked, striding through the crowds with her head down.

"She encountered a beast who was asexual, and it wiped her out at once."

"And *there's* the reason to diversify one's skill set," Liv stated.

"Yes, maybe. But showing a bit of thigh wouldn't hurt you."

"If you make another ridiculous suggestion, I will hurt you," Liv threatened.

He held up his hands in surrender. "Fine, I'll stop trying to help you improve your life. I realize that you prefer boring and practical things. Speaking of which, how is your brother Clark? He seemed to take a real liking to me at the party you urged me to attend."

Liv shook her head as she continued making her way to the brownies' official center. "Clark thought you were the worst, and I had no way to dissuade him from this conclusion. And I asked you to stop by to give me a report about the ring. We just happened to be having a party, which you stayed at much too long. And you left your pants in the backroom."

Rudolf laughed good-naturedly. "It was no problem. I didn't mind attending your silly party at all, although next time put me in charge of decorations. The décor was simply atrocious."

"There was none," Liv said dryly.

"Then what were those ugly little boxes and contraptions you had lying all over the place?" Rudolf asked curiously.

"Electronics."

"Oh, well, then at the next party, get rid of those," Rudolf stated with a wide, toothy grin.

"We can't," Liv answered. "It's an electronics repair shop."

"Too bad. You really should have picked a more glamorous job like model or hair stylist or perfume sprayer."

"That's never, ever going to happen," Liv said, scanning the brick wall next to them to locate the right place to open the hidden door to the office.

Rudolf nodded in understanding. "Yes, you're right. You're too pudgy for modeling, I agree. But maybe in your next life."

Liv rolled her eyes, trying her best to ignore the fae who followed her through the crowd.

"And I appreciate you allowing me to sleep in the back room at the shop," Rudolf said cheerily.

"You passed out after a shot of whiskey and no one could wake you," Liv corrected. "We had no choice but to lay you in the back of the shop."

"Yes, mortal drinks are a bit too much for me." He bumped his shoulder into hers, winking. "And good thought about taking off my pants so I could rest more peacefully."

"You did that after you spilled queso all over yourself."

"Then the next morning, I had to rush out to a meeting with some fae who work as drag queens in your neck of the woods," Rudolf said.

"They didn't notice that you were pantsless? Or anyone on the street, for that matter?"

"I never made it there," Rudolf replied. "I got picked up by a nice man in a uniform in a shiny car with cool lights.

He must have known I was still tired from dancing all night with you because he offered me a ride, but unfortunately, he didn't drop me off at my destination."

"First of all, we didn't dance," Liv said. "And second, how did you get out of jail?"

Rudolf blinked at her dully. "That was jail? I just thought it was a really low-end hotel. That explains why they didn't turn down my bed when I requested it."

"And locked you in a cell?" Liv asked.

"Yes, but I thought that was for kinky purposes. Anyway, the joke's on them, because I simply portaled out of there without leaving a generous tip," Rudolf answered.

"But you *did* tip?" Liv questioned.

He scoffed at her. "Of course. What, do you think I'm a stingy gnome?"

As luck would have it, a group of gnomes passed as Rudolf said that, and they all spat in their direction, holding up their fists. "You know, at some point, I will have to form a diplomatic alliance with the gnomes, and you aren't making my job easy."

"Oh, are you referring to that silly Father Time business?" Rudolf asked. "That man never remembers anything, and that was ages ago."

"It was last week," Liv corrected. "And he's the Father of freaking Time. He sort of *does* remember everything."

Rudolf dismissed her with a shake of his head.

"Are you going to tell me now why you stole that purple gemstone from Papa Creola?" Liv asked, cutting around a group of elves.

"No, but I *am* going to tell you that I'm that much closer

to figuring out the memory connected to your ring," Rudolf said.

"Cool. What is it?" Liv asked.

He shook his head. "I need just a bit longer. I booked a beautiful Airbnb on the coast for us. After a long weekend of passion—"

"The law be damned," Liv cut him off. "I will murder you right here."

He sighed. "Fine. I'll stay in the Airbnb without you. Ocean breezes and Waves help me think."

"Yes, waves have that effect on me, too," Liv related.

He shook his head. "No, I was referring to a stripper from Venice Beach I invited. Her name is Waves."

"Ewww," Liv said. "And you invited *me* to this beach shack too?"

"Well, yes. The more, the merrier."

"No," Liv answered. "The more, the more STDs."

Rudolf halted when Liv did, staring at the blank brick wall. "So you're off to see the brownies again. This is your third or fourth time. Do you have a thing for short guys? If so, that explains why you don't like me."

"I don't like you because you're as scummy as a urinal at a truck stop."

Rudolf nodded. "I agree that pushing me away is for the best. Otherwise, I'll only break your heart. But no matter what you say, I know your true feelings for me. And although I can't return them, the flattery is very nice."

Liv ignored him, stepping forward to announce her presence to the brownies, hoping they'd open the door for her as they'd done before.

"Liv Beaufont, Warrior for the House of Seven, here to

see Mortimer," she called like a weirdo to the solid brick wall.

Rudolf shook his head and clicked his tongue. "I really took you as the type to fall for your own kind, but I'm not one to judge. If you fancy those hairy little cleaners, then you have my full support. I'll even attend the wedding, although I daresay the attention will all be on me and not you as the bride."

"Please note that I'm never, ever getting married, and if by some strange token I actually do, your invitation will be lost in the mail," Liv stated.

Rudolf chuckled. "I do love the way you plan in advance."

The door to the brownie office materialized with a note taped to the front. It read You're most welcome to enter, Liv Beaufont, Warrior for the House of Seven. Please leave the fae at the door. We don't want trash in here.

Rudolf nodded after reading it. "Please tell my friend Mortimer that although I appreciate his offer, I'm much too busy to grace him with my presence. I'm off to the beach cottage to do your bidding and find the memory you so desire."

"Okay," Liv stated. "You know where to find me when you're done."

"And I accept that informal invitation to slip into your bed some night," Rudolf said, hurrying away through the crowd before Liv could protest.

CHAPTER SEVEN

If it were possible, the hallway that led to Mortimer's office was even dustier than before. Liv bent over, trying to keep her hair out of the many cobwebs blanketing the ceiling. She ducked into the official's office, unsurprised to find it overflowing with messy stacks of paper. Mortimer was sitting behind his desk, squinting into a hand mirror.

"Ummm, hello," Liv said to get his attention.

He waved at her to sit down in the tiny chair in front of his desk, not taking his eyes off the mirror. "Do you think I'm overly hairy?"

Liv froze halfway through the process of trying to sit down. "Ummm, I'm not sure I'm in the best position to answer that question. I've only met two brownies."

Mortimer dropped the mirror on his desk and frowned. "I meant for any type of creature."

Liv tried her best to wedge her butt into the chair, keeping most of her weight on her heels. "You really shouldn't let that dumb fae get into your head. He doesn't know what he's talking about."

"Although that may be true, Rudolfus is considered one of the most attractive fae, which makes him one of the most attractive creatures on this planet."

Liv shook her head. "Yes, but you realize his personality counts against him, right?"

He nodded. "I wouldn't want to sit across a dinner table from him, but I don't mind staring at the man."

Liv sighed. "Believe me, he is even more unattractive when he eats. You should have seen him with queso running down his chin. He wasn't a lady's man then."

"You and Rudolfus have been spending much time together, I've heard," Mortimer said.

The brownie had eyes everywhere and probably knew that Rudolf had attended the party at John's shop. That was why she thought he might be able to offer a clue about the demons. "We're working together on something, that's all."

"Yes, Liv Beaufont, Warrior for the House of Seven, has indeed been working on many projects," Mortimer observed. "I've heard tales of your adventures. But what brings you here today? John is happy with our work, isn't he?"

Liv nodded at once. "Oh, yes. He's supremely happy, and so am I. It makes my life easier too that your brownies clean the shop every night. Thank you. I'm actually here to see if you can offer me any information on a specific creature who is fairly mysterious and hard to track down."

Mortimer's face brightened with curiosity. "We have seen lots of creatures. I'm sure I can be of help. Are you looking for a unicorn that goes by the name Blisters? He's always hiding, but I know where to find him, although it isn't technically on Earth. Oh! Let me guess, it's a Londil you're looking for. Those aliens may not be present on this planet, but I know where to find them. We have eyes everywhere."

Liv didn't know what to say for a moment. "Aliens are real?"

Mortimer paused, maybe waiting for her to say she was just kidding. After a few seconds, he laughed. "You're very silly, Liv Beaufont. We all know that aliens are real. Not magical like us, but unique in their own ways."

"Right," Liv said, drawing out the one word to give her time to assimilate this new information. "And no, this isn't about some delightful unicorn or mysterious aliens."

Mortimer scowled. "Unicorns aren't all rainbows and sunshine. They're pretty high-maintenance, if you ask me, and not as useful as most make them out to be. Just go down to their central office, and you'll see what I mean. Unorganized, and totally obsessed with themselves."

Liv tried to keep her gaze off the mirror in front of Mortimer or the dozens of stacks of paper around the office. "I'll take your word for it. Anyway, I'm actually looking for a specific demon."

Mortimer gasped and pushed away from his desk, like trying to put as much space between him and Liv as possible. "Why would you want to know where a specific demon is? I hope it's so that you can avoid it."

Liv shook her head. "Actually, so I can track him down and take his blood."

Mortimer shook his head rather forcefully. "I beseech you to reconsider. There is no reason to put yourself in that kind of danger. The brownies like you. We want to keep you around."

Liv smiled. "I appreciate that, but I have a friend who needs my help. Do you have any information on demons and where to find specific ones? I'm looking for one by the name of Sabatore."

Mortimer was shaking his head before she was even done speaking. "I'm afraid on this matter, I can be of no help. Demons do go after mortals, but usually not the ones we serve. They are two different types of clientele. Ours are genuine and pure, which are two traits a demon doesn't look for."

"Yes, they want the lost and lonely, isn't that right?" Liv asked.

"That's correct," Mortimer answered. "So, as you can see, of all the creatures you could have asked about, those are the ones I can tell you the least of."

Liv sighed, wondering what options they had left. Stefan was running out of time.

"However, my role working with many types has given me certain knowledge that might be of use to you."

Liv perked up, watching as Mortimer began digging into his messy desk drawer. Bits of paper spilled onto the floor as he dug deeper.

"Where is that card?" he muttered, nearly disappearing into the open drawer. "Eureka!" Mortimer held up a yellowed card, his face ecstatic. "Once again, my filing system has proven most useful."

Liv stared around at the towering piles of papers and managed a nod.

"I once met an elf by the name of Renswick," Mortimer

explained, handing the card to her. "A very strange fella. Not the kind of person you'd invite to your parents' house." He snapped his mouth shut, remorse covering his face at once. "I'm sorry, Liv Beaufont. That was very insensitive of me."

She shook her head, dismissing it. "I know what you mean. Please go on."

"Well, Renswick might be very eccentric, but I believe at his core, he's a good person, which is why I'm giving you him as a contact."

Liv studied the card. It read:

Renswick Shoshawnawalla
Ashland, Oregon

"This elf," Liv began. "You think he might know something about Sabatore?"

Mortimer shrugged. "I can't say for certain, but if anyone does, it will be him."

"Renswick Shoshawnawalla," Liv said, reading the card. "That's quite the mouthful. Does he go by Ren for short?"

Mortimer's eyes enlarged. "I wouldn't advise you to call him that. For some reason, he's acted highly offended on the occasions that he's been called that."

"So, this Renswick," Liv began. "Can you tell me more about him?"

"He studies demons," Mortimer explained. "I hear that he has the most extensive catalog of the various individuals, mostly including those who have been around for a long time and have achieved legendary status."

"Why would anyone want to study demons?" Liv asked.

"I had the same thought as you when I learned about it," Mortimer answered. "However, all things in life should be studied by someone so that we understand them better. I don't want to study natural disasters, but I'm grateful that someone does, so we know how to prepare for them. I'm not sure what Renswick's motivation is for studying demons, but if anyone knows where your Sabatore is, it will be that elf."

Liv nodded, trying not to allow herself to hope too much just yet. "How do I find him? It just has a city and state listed here."

Mortimer nodded in understanding. "The area isn't large, and Renswick is well-known there. He lives among the strangest of strange types of people. Just ask around and someone should be able to point you in the direction of his manor, which I hear is pretty spectacular on its own."

"These people…" Liv said, hesitation in her voice. "You say they are strange. Are they dangerous?"

Mortimer shook his head. "No, but you might find them mildly annoying. The city is made up of the north-western tribe of elves, and those are a special brand."

"Oh. A special brand? What does that mean?"

Mortimer gave her a sideways look. "They're all hippies."

CHAPTER EIGHT

"Do you know anything about these eccentric hippies in Oregon?" Liv asked Plato, turning Renswick's card over in her hands, thinking that an address or more information might appear on the other side. It was still blank.

Plato lifted his head off his paws. "I make it a rule to limit my time with elves. Especially ones described as hippies."

"Oh, what's your beef with elves?"

"Nothing," Plato said. "I just spent a better part of a cent —" He caught himself and looked to the side. "I mean, I spent some time with the tribe in the Pacific. I'm still detoxing after the experience."

"What's the tribe like there? Is that in Hawaii?"

Plato nodded. "Yes, and they are all surfers. If I smell suntan lotion again in this lifetime, it will be too soon."

"So, how many lives have you lived?" Liv asked slyly.

"More than one and less than nine," he answered, making Liv laugh out loud.

John danced through from the door in the back, nodding his head along with one of his favorite Beatles songs, *Blackbird*.

"What are you laughing about?" he asked, looking around as if expecting her to be with a customer.

Liv pointed to Plato. "He made an especially funny joke."

The feline had laid his head on his paws and was pretending to be asleep.

John nodded, giving her his usual skeptical expression when she stated that Plato could talk. "Right." He looked down at Pickles, who was trotting beside him. "This little puppy keeps me in stitches, so I know what you mean."

Liv shook her head. "He can talk. I promise."

John didn't seem to hear her as he cued up another song on his jukebox, moving his shoulders as he did. It had quickly become his favorite thing in the store, which made Liv happy. "Have you finished fixing the hairdryer Mrs. Johnson brought in?"

"Oh, I got that fixed ages ago," Liv said, striding over to the shelves.

"And how about the three different vacuum cleaners we got in this morning?" John questioned.

"Yep, those are all good." Liv moved around various items on the shelf, trying to find the devices she'd repaired that morning. "The thing is, we got in a ton of stuff the last week."

John nodded, moving his feet to *Love Me Do*. "Yes, business is bustling. I couldn't be happier. I think it has something to do with the new energy in here. It's...happier."

Liv smiled. "*You're* happier, and it's contagious. The customers love it."

John swayed and Pickles barked, enjoying the dancing. "Well, whatever it is, I'm thrilled."

"I'm glad, but we're running out of places for all the devices," Liv began. "Even the back is full."

"It's a good problem to have," John said. "Never in thirty years do I remember being able to say I had too much work. But with your help, it's not too much. Just enough."

"I'm glad, but I think we have a new problem." Liv squinted, trying to see what was on the back of the shelf. "I can't find anything. There's just too much here, and it's all crammed together."

"Do you think we need a better organization system?" John asked, his mood not altered from this news.

"I think that we need to expand the shop," Liv stated.

John froze. "But the laundromat on the other side has been there for ages. And the deli on the other side, well, I love the Thomasons. And I can't even dream of moving."

Liv held up her finger. "No, I mean magically expanding. There are spells that magicians, especially the giants, use to fit more into less, like the book that Rory gave me." She indicated *Mysterious Creatures*, which was sitting on the workbench. It was almost always by her side. "Giants aren't into making things look better than they are, like magicians do with their homes, but a simple renovation spell could do the trick."

"Do you know how to do such a thing?" John asked.

Liv deflated. "I'm afraid I don't, but I'll learn if you agree to the change."

John thought for a moment. "It would be nice to have

more shelf space in here, but you're already taxed with multiple jobs like tracking down specters or whatever they are."

"Demons," Liv corrected with a giggle.

John grimaced. "Still don't like the idea that you have to hunt such horrible things. I don't know what they are entirely, only what mortal fiction says about them, and it's not good."

Liv nodded. "I'm certain they are much worse in real life than the books, but don't worry. Bellator keeps me safe."

"I'm grateful for that," John stated. "Didn't you say that House of Seven uses one of those spells to hide its size?"

"Yes, the entrance to it in Santa Monica looks like a rundown two-story palm-reading shop," Liv explained.

"And the actual building?" John asked.

"It's seven stories, and quite extensive," Liv said, her heart starting to race just from thinking about the building. "And there are large grounds that include a huge garden. The library takes up an entire floor, although it's three stories most of the time."

"Most of the time?" John questioned, his brow furrowing.

"Well, it changes depending on... Well, I'm not sure what are the factors that influence the library are," Liv stated. "My parents used to say that it was more alive than the garden. If you're not careful, you can easily get lost in there. Apparently, there is still a magician in there who went searching for a book on dragons over a decade ago, and no one has seen him since."

John laughed. "What an incredible place. I'm not sure

why you choose to live in that crummy apartment instead of at the House of Seven."

Liv shot him a look of offense. "Take that back, John Carraway. My apartment isn't crummy. It's awesome and perfect for me, and I can clean it in under ten minutes."

"You could clean it in under ten seconds if you used magic," John corrected.

She laughed now. "That's true, but I'm trying to stay humble."

"And I'm glad you still like your apartment," John said. "If you want to do some renovations to the shop, I'm not going to decline. Business is great, and I don't want to lose the momentum."

Liv put her finger to her lips, thinking of how to use an expansion spell. She didn't want to get this wrong, or she could blow a hole in the wall or make a whole shelf of appliances disappear.

The front door of the shop chimed as Clark entered. He was wearing his usual overly starched pinstripe suit and long dragonhide cape. Today he was sporting a cane with a silver lion's head and wearing an irritated expression on his face.

"Hey, the old man down the block called and said he wants his cane back," Liv joked.

He didn't laugh. "You took Sophia out of the House!"

Liv reared back, not expecting this outburst. "I did, but only to go to Rory's house."

John, probably sensing that things were going to get heated, acted as if he were looking for something and it was undoubtedly in the back of the shop.

"That's even worse," Clark nearly yelled, getting control

of his anger. "A giant's house. That's where you took our little sister. You realize that giants hate us?"

"Not Rory," Liv argued. "Well, he hates us less than the other giants, anyway."

"It doesn't matter," Clark said, his cheeks flushing red. "Sophia is young, but she has her magic. It's not safe for her to be out of the House."

"That's no life for her to live," Liv countered. "You know that Mom and Dad would have never approved of locking her up."

Clark sighed. "Mom and Dad aren't here. They're dead, and we're the ones who are supposed to be caring for Sophia now. Well, actually that was left on me because you abandoned us."

Now it was all coming out. Liv stood, feeling the anger vibrate in her. "I didn't abandon you. I left because I couldn't stand to be in the House of Seven. Everywhere I looked it reminded me of them. And I argued that there was something not right about their deaths and no one would listen. I couldn't take it anymore, so yes, I left, but I didn't abandon my family. When you needed me, what did I do?"

Clark simmered for a moment, his eyes buzzing with stress. "You came back, but that doesn't excuse that you left in the first place. And I've been given the role of caring for Sophia, and she's not to leave the House again. I shouldn't have even brought her here for the party."

"Clark, she might be young, but she's not incompetent—"

"I know that, Liv," he cut her off. "That's why she has to be protected. If anyone knew what she was capable of...

Well, I don't even want to think about it. They could try to take her from us."

"I'd never allow that to happen," Liv snapped. "There are only a few people I'd lay down my life for, but that little girl is at the very top of the list."

Clark laughed dryly. "That list is long, actually. Who do you think you're fooling? And that's another excellent point. You're a Warrior with a ton of enemies. Sophia isn't safe leaving the House with you."

"She's much safer with me than with you. You wouldn't even know how to fight a hungry cockroach," Liv spat.

"I would too," Clark fired.

"And she's *my* sister too. She needs to see the world, not just read about it in books. Because she's so powerful, it's even more important that we train her and expose her to things."

"Liv, I hear what you're saying," Clark said, seeming to settle down slightly. "Do you think I like keeping her locked up? I'm so busy with the council now that I can't take her out. And before I was appointed, I was busy studying. I wished there was more time. That the world was a better place. That she could run and play outside like other children. But Sophia isn't normal. She's extraordinary, and that means she has to be protected."

"I agree, and the best way to protect her is to teach her," Liv stated.

"Liv…"

"Will you stop saying my name? You only ever say it when you're mad at me, which is conditioning me to hate my name."

Clark actually laughed at this. "Yeah, you're right. Sorry. It's a habit."

"Look, I appreciate that you want Sophia to be safe, and I know the responsibility fell on you because I was gone. But I'm back now, and you don't have to raise her on your own. We don't have to fully agree on everything, but please let me be a part of this. Don't shut me out just because you don't agree with my ideas."

Clark thought about that for a moment. "I don't want you taking her out of the House without me knowing."

Liv nodded. "Fair enough. But I want her to leave the House sometimes."

Clark let out a heavy breath. "Fine, but we have to discuss where she's going. And she has to be supervised at all times. And she can't do magic when she leaves. And I don't want her out past dark."

"Is 'she is to have no fun' on that list too?"

"Ha-ha," Clark said, not amused.

They were quiet for a moment. Clark softened a bit, and Liv hoped he'd quit staring at her. Finally, he said, "I've missed you, Liv."

She smiled. "Thanks. I've missed you, sort of."

He laughed. "You're the only one who really ever argued with me."

"That's because you're always wrong," Liv fired back at him.

"I'm not. But Ian never cared enough to argue with me, and Reese didn't know better. And Mom and Dad, well, they…"

"Only ever loved you, showering you with praise you didn't deserve."

He shook his head at her. "That's low, but you're right. They were only ever supportive of us. I'm pretty certain if you said you wanted to run away with the circus, they would have encouraged the idea."

"They would have dashed out and bought me a leotard," Liv said. She pointed to the cane. "Seriously, what's up with that, old man?"

He held up the cane, which was rich in detail. "It's a weapon. I brought it along in case I needed it."

"Needed it?" Liv asked.

Clark looked around with a paranoid expression on his face. "We're getting closer to, well, whatever Ian and Reese wanted us to find out. And you know what happened to them. I'm worried—"

"That whoever murdered them and Mom and Dad will come after us?" Liv asked. "I can guarantee they will. But we're being careful for now, so don't worry."

He nodded. "It's just, this business with the mortal and magician war has me really stressed. I've been doing research nonstop since you told me that, and I can't find anything to support it. How in the world could an entire war be erased from history?"

Liv shrugged. "I don't know, but whoever is covering things up has gone to great lengths. Rudolf says he's lost memories connected to the ring. The names of the Founders are hidden in the ancient chamber, the only place they reside. There is a lot we don't know, and it's been hidden very carefully."

"Which is why we have to be more cautious than ever," Clark stated. "This is big, and someone has gone to great lengths to keep it buried."

"Don't worry," Liv replied. "We'll be okay. But how does your cane work? Is there a sword hidden inside?"

Clark looked at it funny. "No, it's just a magic cane with various powers. Mostly keeps me from getting my hands dirty."

"Because obviously that would kill you," Liv said with a laugh.

He joined in, not looking as tense as before. "Obviously."

Liv's eyes darted to the crammed shelves. "Hey, do you by chance know how to do expansion magic and other ones related to sprucing up spaces?"

He gawked at her. "What's my name?"

"Dumbface?" she shot back.

He poked his tongue out at her. "And yes. Of course, I do. Every preschooler does."

"Ha-ha," Liv said. "I missed that day of school." She indicated the shelves. "Would you mind helping me with a project and teaching me at the same time? I want to make this place look better."

"Are you asking for my help?" Clark asked in disbelief.

"Yes, but don't tell anyone or I'll die from mortification."

He pointed the cane at the shelves with a smile. "Your secret is safe with me, Liv."

CHAPTER NINE

Stefan ran the whetstone over the edge of the sword's blade, producing a noise that made Liv flinch. That was probably for the best since it covered her initial reaction when she saw him in the dark alley waiting for her. He looked like absolute hell. His usually bright blue eyes were dull and more sunken than the last time she saw him, which now that she thought about, wasn't that long ago. His face was hollow in places, and he'd definitely lost weight. Worse than all of that was the shifty expression in his eyes, like one would see on a homeless person who was dealing with a serious internal battle.

Liv didn't expect a cheery greeting when she strode in Stefan's direction, but she also hadn't expected the growl that rolled out of his throat. She slid her hand to the hilt of her sword, ready to pull it if necessary.

Stefan's eyes followed her movement. He shook his head as if trying to come back to himself. "I'm sorry, I..."

"Are you all right?" Liv asked.

He nodded and then corrected the movement, shaking his head. "No. I think you need to finish me off."

Liv gulped, wishing he'd laugh and say that was a joke. She knew it wasn't.

"You still have time," Liv said. "And I found a lead."

To her relief, his face brightened slightly. "Oh?"

"Yes. I might have found someone who knows where Sabatore could be," she explained.

The hope in his eyes vanished. "I was hoping you'd found Sabatore."

"Well, this could get us one step closer, and I promise to be fast. Do you want to go with me?" Liv asked.

Stefan returned to sharpening his sword. "No, I think I'm better off hunting demons. At least I can be of service —until I'm not."

Liv's eyes closed for a half-beat. This was harder than she expected. It wasn't that she cared about Stefan Ludwig; she just didn't want him to die. In the beginning, she hadn't trusted him at all, thinking he was some egotistical Warrior who blindly did what the council ordered, but then she had gotten to know him, and he wasn't anything like what she'd expected. He was egotistical at times, but he was also brave and self-sacrificing and talented in ways that constantly surprised her.

So maybe I do care about him, she thought to herself.

"Are you sure you want to keep hunting?" Liv asked, careful to keep her eyes off his hands, which were shaking as he ran the stone over the blade.

He nodded. "It actually helps. Reminds me that I'm still human, although it's difficult sometimes to finish the job by killing them. But I think it's good for me. Hopefully, the longer I keep hunting, the longer I postpone...well, you know."

"But you said before that you felt more akin to the demons than magicians," Liv dared to say. There was no point in skirting around the truth.

"Yeah, I know. But I'm only going to slow you down and cause unnecessary attention if I go with you," Stefan stated. "I'll just lay low, mostly. Try to kill a demon here and there when I have the energy."

"Okay, well, like I said, I'll be fast. Let's plan to meet back up tomorrow morning first thing."

He nodded, pointing to Bellator. "Tell me, why don't you ever have to sharpen your sword? Is that one of the properties of it being giant-made?"

Liv eyed Bellator and nodded. "Yes, it never dulls or rusts. It's also supposed to offer me special abilities in battle, but I don't know what those are yet. Maybe I'm not bonded with it closely enough yet."

Liv withdrew the sword and offered it to Stefan. "Do you want to take it, since you're going after demons?"

He considered the offer but shook his head, his usually spikey hair falling down over one eye. "No, no one but you should swing your sword. But I appreciate the idea. And you're never going to bond with the sword fully if you loan it out."

"It just felt like the practical approach," Liv reasoned, although she wasn't entirely sure why she'd made the offer. Maybe it was out of pity.

"Your sword must be your constant companion," Stefan said, regarding his own weapon, which was much larger than Bellator. "It's an extension of you.

Once you establish that, the benefits it offers will be obvious."

"Akio said the same thing about it being an extension," Liv supplied. "I get that now when I'm fighting with Bellator."

Stefan stood suddenly, some of his old speed surfacing. He was close to Liv, his eyes burning. "An inexperienced Warrior believes they only need their sword when fighting. However, your sword should be so much more than a weapon. It should be your compass, your guide, a clue when you're lost, and your strength when you're weak. If you bond with that sword, you'll find it to be most valuable to you when you're not using it to fight."

Liv nodded, taken aback by how different Stefan was at that moment. He might have been holding onto his humanity by only a thread, but he was more lucid than she'd seen him recently. It was like something had been stirred in him, bringing his great wisdom to the surface momentarily.

"Okay, we'll meet here tomorrow," Liv finally said, backing away.

"Yes, tomorrow," he affirmed.

Liv opened a portal to Ashland, Oregon, realizing there wasn't much time before sunset.

"And Liv?" Stefan said from behind her.

She turned, giving him a questioning look.

"If I'm not here tomorrow, come looking for me and do what has to be done."

Liv gulped. Nodded. Averted her eyes from his as she stepped through the portal.

CHAPTER TEN

The smell of rain was fresh in the air when Liv stepped through the portal onto a charming street in downtown Ashland, Oregon. The city was nestled in a tight, tree-lined valley, the green mountains making her feel like she was snuggled in a cozy blanket. The frigid wind that hit her in the face immediately contradicted that.

Liv pulled her hood over her head as she looked around the street, which was filled with boutiques and cafes. There were bright colors everywhere, as if the paint store had had a sale on primary hues. She was about to duck into a coffee shop to ask about Renswick when she noticed a park on the other side of a small plaza. The lush grass and autumn leaves weren't what attracted her attention, though. It was the various characters wearing dreadlocks and baggy pants, some of them holding instruments and others dancing around or braiding each other's hair.

"Bingo," Liv muttered to herself, making her way over to the hippies on the grass. Even though their ears were glamoured, Liv knew they were elves. She'd started to notice that elves moved with a unique grace. They also were long and lanky, and usually had angular features.

As she approached, one of the men held out his arms. He had a long beard filled with colorful beads. The facial hair made him look much older than he was by mortal standards.

"Free hug," he offered Liv. "They cost us nothing and give us so much. Studies show that twenty seconds is the perfect amount of time to hug. That's when the medical benefits kick in."

"Ummm...no," Liv said, shaking her head at him.

Undeterred, he kept his arms wide, like she might change her mind at any time and he'd be ready for the embrace.

"I'm actually looking for someone and thought you all might be able to help," Liv continued, having to speak loud to be heard over the guitar music.

"We're all looking for someone," a woman said, pulling up one of her feet and resting it on the inside of her leg, hands meeting in prayer as she balanced on one foot.

"Yes, well, I'm looking for someone specific, and I heard you all might be able to point me in the right direction," Liv stated.

"It's not often that we have a magician join us," a man holding a guitar said, continuing to strum the strings. "Take a seat and let's celebrate our uniqueness."

"I'm actually on a tight schedule," Liv stated.

The hippies gave each other a collective nod. "Magicians are always rushing and going. Never able to live in the moment. If you're not careful, life will pass you by."

Liv wanted to tell them that they could frolic and braid

each other's hair in the park because she and other magicians were out keeping the streets safe from demons and other monsters, but she knew better than to try to reason with a hippie. The hemp seed oil they used instead of soap obviously had killed most of their brain cells, making it impossible to have a logical conversation.

"I'm looking for Renswick Shoshawnawala. Can one of you point me in the right direction?"

The circle of elves fell suddenly silent.

The hippie who had offered her a hug dropped his arms, giving her a disappointed stare. "Renswick doesn't like to have visitors. He doesn't celebrate free love like we do. You'd be better off hanging out with us."

"We're about to put up a slackline and practice becoming one with the invisible force that connects us all," the woman doing yoga said. "Why don't you stick around for that?"

"Actually, I've been doing my own slacklining all day long," Liv lied. "All tuckered out. What I really need is to speak with Renswick." Liv pointed to the various large Victorian houses surrounding the park. "Does he live in one of these?" Mortimer had said that the house was impressive, and all of the ones here were bold and beautiful.

The guy with the guitar shook his head. "No, Renswick lives right there." He pointed to an empty lot on a nearby hill covered in evergreens.

Liv blinked, thinking the fading sunlight was playing tricks on her. She was about to declare that she didn't see anything when a house that more closely resembled a church materialized. It was a gothic Victorian, with many spires and unique attention to detail. Gargoyles perched on various places of the roof, which was covered with spikes. The house was painted in varying shades of grays and black. There was only one light on in the entire building—on the third floor at the top of the tallest tower.

Liv wasn't sure why, but she shivered, feeling a deep chill at her core.

"Renswick doesn't leave his house, and he doesn't allow visitors," the girl explained.

"But I have to see him," Liv said adamantly. "It's really important."

"We've tried to include him, but he says that our ways are frivolous and a waste of time," the free-hugging hippie shared.

Liv already liked Renswick better than the rest of them. "Can one of you please help me get a meeting with him?"

They laughed like they were suddenly drunk on cherry wine.

"I'm afraid we'd only hurt your chances with Renswick," the woman told her.

"Well, it's really important that I speak to him. Do you have any suggestions?" Liv asked.

The hippie with the guitar smiled. "Don't worry. All you have to do is make it past his guards. Then he'll see you."

"Guards?" Liv questioned. "Does he have a dog or something?"

The hippies blinked at her in surprise. "No, you can see the guards clearly from here."

Liv scanned the house, seeing nothing but the building and the gargoyles that adorned it. Then it dawned on her. "Wait, are you saying that the gargoyles are the guards?"

The hippies laughed. "Of course they are," the woman said.

"And how do I get past them?" Liv asked.

The guy with the guitar shrugged. "It's been a long time since anyone has dared to take on the challenge. What was his name? Thorn?"

They all nodded.

"Yes, Thorn was the last one to try to go in there," the woman stated.

"And what happened to him?" Liv asked.

"He's floating with the birds."

"Wow, Renswick killed him for knocking at his door?" Liv questioned.

"Oh no," the guy with beads in his beard said. "He's just gone insane. He spends most days floating in the lake, paddling around next to the ducks."

"What did Renswick do to him?"

The hippies looked at each other for an answer. When no one supplied one, they directed their gaze at Liv and shrugged.

In pure hippie fashion, they'd been only mildly helpful, leaving Liv with more questions than answers. Still, she made up her mind to set off for the large gothic house, wishing she knew what she was getting herself into. Risking her sanity to talk to an eccentric elf about demons didn't seem like the smartest thing she'd done in a while, but she couldn't let Stefan down.

She took a tentative step in the direction of the house, looking at the hippies. "Thanks for your help. Wish me luck."

"There's no such thing as luck, but depending on your

zodiac, you might need to wait until Mars moves into your eighth house, conjoining you with unexpected outcomes to life's problems," the woman imparted.

"Yeah, thanks," Liv said, shaking her head at the elves. "I think I'll try my hand at luck anyway."

CHAPTER ELEVEN

"Why can't I ever be sent to some normal person for help?" Liv asked Plato, looking up at the dark house towering in front of her.

"Because you didn't go into accounting," he answered.

"I didn't go into magic, either. It sort of chose me." The handle on the wrought iron gate screeched when Liv lifted it. "So, what do you make of this place?"

"It's haunted, for one," Plato said, following her as she entered the yard.

Looking back at the park, she noticed the elves all watching her with interest. She waved sarcastically at them, plastering a giant fake grin on her face.

"I think the hippies took a liking to you," Plato observed, looking back as the group waved cheerfully back at Liv.

"That's good, I guess. I don't need any more enemies."

"Yes, and rumor has it that if you piss off a hippie, you're cursed to have GMOs in your food for eternity," Plato joked.

Liv gave him a proud smile. "Nice one." Directing her attention to the house again, Liv pushed her hood onto her shoulders. "Haunted, you say? I ain't afraid of no ghosts."

"I wouldn't be either," Plato began. "However, poltergeists aren't as delightful."

Liv froze. She didn't have any experience with poltergeists. "Wait, I thought the guards were gargoyles?"

Plato indicated the corner of the yard with his head. "I think it's both. Incoming."

A small boulder was rolling through the air in Liv's direction, headed straight for her. She did the first thing she could think of and dropped to the soggy earth, her fingers pressing into the soft dirt. The boulder rushed over her head, turning around when it got to the other side of the yard. Like a bull about to charge, it rotated and sped forward again, appearing to build up speed.

Liv gave Plato an annoyed look. "Must be nice to be short right now."

"It is," he agreed. "It's even better that I can do *this*." The lynx disappeared, leaving Liv alone in the yard.

She sighed, pushing to her feet and directing her hand at the boulder speeding in her direction. It exploded into a hundred tiny pieces, sending debris all over the place. Liv shielded her face from the dust as applause broke out from the park. She chanced a look, to find the hippies all cheering her on, having seen her nearly not escape the mad boulder.

Liv managed a smile in return, keeping her attention on the yard. She was expecting another rock to be flung at her, but a cracking noise overhead stole her attention. Liv glanced up. The stone gargoyles were looking down at her, their wings flapping like they might take off at any moment.

The door to the house was only fifteen yards away. Liv debated making a run for it, but she didn't want to be trapped on the porch if she couldn't easily defeat the four gargoyles glaring down at her. That was when she noticed words etched over the front of the porch. She squinted, reading aloud:

"That which you resist persists."

Was this a riddle or just Renswick's favorite quote? Liv wasn't sure, but she figured she'd take the direct approach with his guards.

"Hey there," Liv sang. "I'm just here to see Renswick. Totally not a big deal. Is it cool if I just knock at the door?"

The closest gargoyle opened his mouth and leaned over the edge of the roof. Liv wasn't sure if it was going to say something in response to her question. It wasn't.

Fire streamed from the gargoyle's mouth, shooting straight at her. A second time, Liv dove out of the way, doing a front roll to avoid the flames.

The hippies yelled from the park, switching from worry to relief when it was clear that Liv hadn't been harmed.

A gargoyle lifted off the corner of the house, diving in her direction with its large stone wings flapping.

Liv didn't think that ducking a third time would get her out of this mess. Pulling out Bellator, she stood strong. The flying gargoyle sped up, its black eyes narrowed on her. Liv didn't budge from her spot, just tightened her grip on Bellator. When the gargoyle swept by her, claws extended, Liv swung the sword at it, and the metal clanged on the stone. Unharmed, the gargoyle flew back up to the top of the house. Beside it, two more gargoyles materialized.

Wait, what, Liv thought. *They're multiplying?*

"Behind you!" the hippies yelled from the park.

Liv stooped and spun around just in time to see a tombstone rising into the air, bringing up clumps of mud as it lifted free from the ground. Swinging a sword at a giant tombstone seemed like a dumb idea, so Liv did the only other thing she could think of. She ran.

She darted toward the side of the yard, which was overgrown and filled with many other stones. After she'd hurdled over several slabs, she realized this was a cemetery.

Gross, she thought. Who builds their house on top of a cemetery? And then a different thought occurred to her. What if the house was there first and the graves were new additions? What if they were people who had tried to get past the guards and failed?

Liv heard something moving fast behind her and glanced over her shoulder to see not only the tombstone but also two gargoyles racing in her direction. She considered using the same spell she had on the boulder, but it didn't feel right to blast a tombstone into pieces.

In her hands, she felt Bellator tug. At first, she thought it was a trick of her imagination, but then it happened again, this time harder, nearly pulling her off her feet, and Liv realized that a mausoleum was beside her. To her surprise the wrought iron gate was half-open, lighted candles illuminating the entrance from the other side. Swerving, Liv sprinted into the building, pressing her back up against the wall. The sounds of movement faded.

Holding Bellator out like a mirror, Liv tried to gauge what was happening outside. The tombstone had halted in midair and was wavering like it was trying to decide what to do next—or rather, the poltergeist that controlled it was.

The gargoyles had landed on the grass and were marching back and forth in front of the mausoleum.

They can't or won't come in here, Liv realized.

She pushed away from the wall, careful to stay out of the doorway. Was it because this was a tomb that they didn't dare enter? Or was there something special about this one?

Taking careful steps to the stone casket in the center of the small tomb, Liv searched for a name. She wiped her fingertips over the cobwebs covering the side of the casket, noticing how many letters there were. Before she had it entirely cleaned off, she already knew what it said: Shoshawnawalla

Liv wondered for a moment if Renswick was a vampire and this was where he spent his days. The waning sunlight meant that if he *was* a vampire, he'd be up soon. She wasn't sure how she felt about that.

Then she noticed the engraved words on the front of the casket. They read, Delilah, May the Peace that Eluded You on Earth Find You in the Afterlife.

Delilah Shoshawnawalla? Liv wondered. *Was that Renswick's mother? Grandmother? Or—*

Bellator twitched in Liv's hand, the point directed up suddenly. She eyed the sword, curious about its new and strange behavior. Had this been what Stefan was talking about when he said swords were useful for other things besides fighting? It did seem to be acting like a compass for her, but she didn't understand how or why. It had pointed her to safety, though, getting her away from the flying tombstone, followed by the stone gargoyles.

Her gaze flew up to where the tip of Bellator was pointing. Above the door were the same words as above the porch: That which you resist persists.

What did that imply? Liv wondered. At face value, she knew what it meant. If you oppose something, you bring it to yourself. But what did it mean in the context of this situation?

Plato appeared beside her, yawning like he hadn't just popped into a mausoleum while gargoyles stalked her outside.

"Where you been?" Liv asked him, looking up as something thudded on the roof.

"Scrapbooking about our latest adventures," he responded, not missing a beat.

A gargoyle knocked on the side of the building, sending dust and dirt raining down from overhead. Liv covered her eyes. "Did you use the album with rose-scented pages I got for you?"

He smirked. "Yes, but I noticed that we don't have very many selfies."

"Many?" Liv questioned as the ground under her shook. The gargoyles weren't happy—that much was clear. They weren't coming in, but something told her that they were hoping to frighten her out.

"We don't have any, actually," Plato corrected.

"Do you want me to pause and take a selfie of us now?" Liv asked, looking around as the gargoyles began circling the building. She didn't want to get trapped, but that was exactly what she'd done.

"I don't think the lighting is quite right for picture-taking in here," Plato said.

"Which is exactly the reason we shouldn't do that in here right now," Liv joked.

"Well, and also, I don't show up on film or camera screens," Plato stated casually.

"Of course you don't," Liv replied dryly. "So, strange cat, do you have any bright ideas on how I can get out of here?"

"Teleport?"

Liv shook her head. "No. I came all this way to talk to this expert on demons. If I leave, Stefan will be that much farther from a solution."

"And if you don't, you'll be that much closer to joining his lady in this box."

Liv pursed her lips. "Show some respect."

"What happened when you tried to battle the gargoyles?" Plato asked.

"Nothing, really," Liv said, spinning around as something rocked the back wall.

"Think, Liv," Plato encouraged, making her pause. She looked down at the cat, realizing he knew the answer but was trying to lead her to it.

"Will you just tell me what the answer to this riddle is?"

He shook his head. "I can't."

"Are you bound by some secrecy act that governs lynx-es?" she joked.

"Exactly," he answered at once.

"I was kidding. That can't really be a thing."

He arched an eyebrow at her.

"Okay, fine. You hide the truth. That's your deal." Liv tapped her leg, trying to think with the constant thudding around the building. "So, when I ran from the gargoyle's fire, that made another one attack me. And then..." The ground vibrated under her feet again, causing the lid on the casket to rattle. "And when I tried to fight the gargoyle, it didn't work, and it multiplied. Then when I ran..." Liv's eyes trailed back up to the phrase over the door. "Are you saying that the longer I resist these gargoyles, the more they are going to come after me? If I fight them, they'll only get worse, multiplying and who knows what else?"

"I don't believe I said anything," Plato said with a smile in his voice.

"That's what you're implying though, aren't you?"

"What do *you* think it means?" Plato asked.

"Well, the gargoyles are meant to protect the house," Liv began slowly, trying to piece it all together, even with the many distractions around the mausoleum. "If someone meant the owner of the house harm, they might try to battle the guards."

"That makes sense to me," Plato said, a leading tone in his voice.

"However, if someone *didn't* mean harm to the owner, then they wouldn't fight back because they'd have no ill will," Liv stated.

The many noises outside the building dissipated, and a strange flapping noise filled the air. Liv stiffened, listening for more.

"So, I need to go out there and ignore the gargoyles?" Liv asked, even though she knew Plato wasn't going to answer her. "If I resist them, they will persist, but if I disregard them, they will go away, allowing me entry."

"Or they might sear off your hair and break you in two," Plato offered.

"Thanks for the vote of confidence," Liv said with a morbid laugh. "I get how this drove that hippie mad. If everything he did only made it worse, I bet he was beside himself with frustration."

"It's a good lesson for life," Plato stated. "What we focus on, we tend to attract more of."

"How does that work for fighting demons and whatnot?" Liv asked.

"Well, I didn't say it was foolproof. It's more about the nature of our thoughts in general."

Liv pursed her lips at him. "I never took you for the pop psychology type."

"Well, then you have a lot to learn. I spent much of the eighties coining terms like 'tough love.'"

"I'm not surprised," Liv said with a laugh. "You're the king of tough love."

The area outside the mausoleum was quiet now, all of the gargoyles seemingly gone back to their perches. "What about the poltergeist? Will it leave me alone if I ignore it?"

Plato tilted his head to the side, giving her a look that said, "What do you think?"

She nodded, filling in the answer. "Yeah, something tells me the poltergeist operates on its own laws, which have more to do with angst and less to do with protecting."

Liv took a step toward the entrance, sheathing Bellator. "Okay, so I just need to go out there and ignore the gargoyles no matter what they throw at me. I can do that. It's just mind over matter, right?"

"It's magic, dear Liv," Plato answered. "Take your mind out of it, and the spell will break."

Liv offered him a smile. "See, you *can* be helpful when you want to be."

He shook his head. "If you tell anyone that, I'll deny it vehemently."

"You don't talk to anyone else, so nice try." Liv winked at him.

"Touché," Plato answered, disappearing at once.

CHAPTER TWELVE

The sun had set when Liv stepped out of the mausoleum. The glow of the moon cascading through the trees provided enough light for her to negotiate the path around the headstones. She kept her gaze directed upward, also listening for any sounds of boulders whizzing toward her.

Liv made it to the front of the yard without a single incident. Possibly infected by the strange optimism of the hippies, she started to think that the obstacles had all been erased and she'd passed the test. All she'd have to do is stroll up to the double doors and knock.

A twig snapped under Liv's boot, and she froze. Hearing the sound of weeds and grass breaking at her back, she chanced a glance behind her and saw yet another stone rushing in her direction. This one was an angel with her wings folded around her body. Without hesitation, Liv directed her hand at the statue, sending a pulse of energy in its direction and breaking it to pieces.

"Seriously, will you just lay off me for five seconds?" she

dared to ask the invisible poltergeist. "Let me deal with the damn gargoyles, and then we can make it a fair fight. I will battle you until we destroy everything in this yard, but one thing at a time."

The sound of grass tearing echoed behind her. Liv turned, expecting to see another stone levitating in the air. Instead, a bundle of weeds and sad dandelions rose, dirt clinging to their roots. They flew over until they were even with Liv's face.

"Is this your way of agreeing to a momentary truce?" she asked, looking around. When there was no answer, she wrapped her hand around the bouquet and feigned a smile. "Thanks."

She tucked the flowers into the pocket of her cape, thinking how strange her life truly was.

The shifting of stones high up on the roof stole her attention. It was time to test Plato's theory. It wasn't that she doubted the cat, but standing idly by as furious gargoyles attacked her would take a bit of faith. The six beasts perched on the edge of the roof, staring down at her with a degree of menace she'd rarely seen before. It was like she'd stolen their lunch and then tossed it down the drain.

Liv's stomach rumbled. Now she was hungry? *What horrible timing,* she thought.

If I get through this, I'll buy myself a burger the size of my face.

As before, the gargoyle on the closest corner of the roof opened its mouth. More than anything, Liv wanted to close her eyes. Actually, more than that, she wanted to run or teleport. Do anything but remain frozen.

Instead, she let her hands hang loosely by her side and stared up at the gargoyle with unblinking eyes. A neat stream of orange fire soared from its mouth straight at her. She felt the blaze of heat as it neared, and for a moment considered that Plato was wrong. How would it look when the House found out she had died without putting up a fight? How would it look that she had died at the home of a strange elf? Her life flashed before her eyes, but in all the wrong ways.

The hippies, who were still in the park, yelled various pieces of advice while they watched this scene by moonlight. "Watch out!" "No!" "Move."

It all happened in slow motion for Liv. Her face warmed, then it was burning hot. The fire was close. Searing her eyes. About to engulf her.

And then it was gone.

She blinked up, trying to make out what had happened. The gargoyle was still perched low, its mouth open, but the fire had disappeared. She gazed down at her cape, expecting to find it scorched. It wasn't. She wasn't burned anywhere, although the residual heat still wafted against her face even with the chilly fog moving across the lawn.

The hippies made muffled sounds of relief at her back, but she didn't dare turn to look at them. Instead, she kept her eyes trained on the gargoyles. They'd moved out of formation and were crawling around on the roof, seemingly patrolling, their eyes darting to her every few seconds.

Without warning, one sped off the rooftop, its stone wings flapping as it circled in the air. Liv had seen this move before and knew what happened next. Her fingers flexed beside Bellator, but she stopped herself from pulling the weapon. Instead, she kept her chin held high and didn't flinch even when the gargoyle switched paths, diving straight at her.

Again the hippies yelled, sounding like a bunch of overly-excited school children. Liv blocked them out, her skin perspiring as the gargoyle drew ever closer.

"What we resist persists," she said aloud, forcing herself to stay still even at the moment right before impact.

The gargoyle flew straight through her like a cold breeze, landing with a thud on the wet grass behind her.

Desperately, Liv wanted to turn around and see what it was doing, but she knew better than to turn her back on the other five gargoyles, who were watching her so intently. So far she'd withstood the test. Plato had been right. This was mind over magic.

The gargoyles huddled together on the roof, looking like a football team deciding on their next play, then one by one, they began to dissolve, disappearing into the night air.

Liv thought she'd finally done it when the last one disappeared. She wiggled her toes in her boots, ready to set off for the door, when something black that was much larger than the gargoyles shot up from the rooftop. Liv blinked, trying to make out the shape of the figure, not sure if it was a beast or a rippling piece of fabric. There was something so different from the gargoyles about it. It didn't move like a monster.

She realized what it was when it stepped into the light. It moved like a man.

It was Adler Sinclair.

CHAPTER THIRTEEN

L iv could hardly believe her eyes as she stared up at the pale magician standing on the third story rooftop, holding a staff. His long white beard rippled in the wind, and his treacherous eyes were screwed up with anger.

Every impulse in her screamed that she should fight. Pull Bellator and make a stand against the threatening force high above her.

Adler raised his staff, muttering incantations that Liv couldn't hear, and she braced herself for what would come next. Although she'd already faced fire and a gargoyle, this was against every instinct. Everything in her told her to fight. To battle what came next. To defend herself.

She expected a bolt of lightning or a blast of fire to surge from his staff. Instead, the magician flew down to the ground, landing beside her and towering over her. Liv was used to looking up at Adler Sinclair, but not like this.

She was defenseless, unable to speak her mind or do

any of the things that usually made her feel empowered against him.

When he spoke, his words echoed in her mind for what felt like a long time.

"I didn't want to kill you, but you leave me no choice," Adler said, his voice a hoarse whisper.

Liv's hands shook by her side. She knew what came next, but it didn't matter. There was nothing to be done. She could only stand by powerless as her enemy struck her down.

Adler lifted his staff and muttered a single spell. Bright light shot out of the end of his staff, directed at Liv, and it hit her in the chest, sending an ache straight to her core.

She'd been wrong.

This would kill her.

She'd stood idly by, not defending herself.

And now she was...

The figure of Adler dissolved into a mound of debris, like the remnants of the statues churned to dust.

Clapping woke her from her reverie. Liv almost dared to look at the park, where she suspected the hippies were still watching her, but she caught a figure standing on the porch of the old house.

He was dressed in a three-piece black and white suit and was wearing a bowtie. His pants looked to be too short for him, showing off a bit of his stark white socks. Actually, Renswick Shoshawnawalla looked like he had just stepped out of a silent film, not just because of the way he was dressed, but in that he too was black and white, as if he'd yet to be colored.

He stopped clapping when Liv noticed him. His black hair was cropped tightly to his head, and his mustache looked like a tiny pencil sitting below his nose. In his eyes was a brooding mischief that was both curious and disconcerting, like he was planning a trick right then.

"Very well done, magician," Renswick said, striding off the porch, his hands now clasped behind his back. "I was certain you'd defend yourself against your evil bad guy, but in the end, you stood brave."

He eyed the mound of dust thoughtfully. "Who is he to you? Your father? A mean uncle? The salesman who sold you that cape?"

Liv glanced down at her traveling cape and grimaced. "What's wrong with this?"

A smile worked at his lips. "Oh, nothing. It just shrieks, 'I'm a magician.'"

"But I *am* a magician," Liv argued.

Renswick rocked forward on his toes and back again on his heels. "That you are. And you've gone to impressive lengths to get my attention, so you have it." He held an arm out, indicating his house. "Would you like to come inside? There's a bite in the air, and the hippies on the lawn won't stop gawking at us."

Liv cast a glance at the park, where the hippies were in fact ogling them in disbelief. "Yes, that would be great. Thank you."

Liv's eyes darted to the small mound of dust on the ground behind her, supposedly the first gargoyle who had charged her, then her eyes swiveled to the pile that was Adler Sinclair.

"How did you know to make it...well, that man?" Liv asked, pointing to where Adler had stood moments prior, looking real and whole.

Renswick held up a finger, a clever glint in his eyes. "Oh, I knew nothing. It's a simple security spell that works by drawing out the intruder's worst enemies—those you most want to fight. You resisted your greatest adversary even as he was about to strike you down. Very impressive —some might say foolish—but it fulfilled the conditions of the test, and therefore I don't see you as harmful to me." He swept his arm toward the house again. "Shall we go in, then?"

Liv nodded, following the elf as he strode off.

When they stepped across the threshold, Renswick held out his hand.

Liv was so distracted by the many overwhelming aspects of the foyer that she hardly registered the gesture.

"I'll take your cape, Ms..."

With her mouth hanging open, Liv eyed the stuffed crow that sat on the banister of the staircase. It had an uncanny resemblance to the one in the Chamber of the Tree, but Liv reasoned that all crows looked alike.

Hanging on the walls were several large oil paintings. Much like Renswick, they were done in black and white, as if the painter didn't have any colors on his palette. The entry was filled with strange gothic-inspired items, such as a grandfather clock with many detailed carvings around the face, a coat rack with no coats, and an umbrella stand without any umbrellas.

Coming back to herself, Liv nodded, taking off her

cape. "Ms. Beaufont," she supplied. "However, you can call me 'Liv.'"

Renswick lifted a sharp black eyebrow as he took her cape. "You are the daughter of Guinevere Beaufont, then?"

Liv knew that her mother had been a Warrior for a long time, supposedly meeting many magical creatures, and yet it always surprised her when she met someone who had known her. It was like she was somehow preserved through their knowledge of her, meaning she was somehow still alive.

"You knew my mother?" Liv asked.

Renswick shook his head. "I have heard of her. You know how people often say someone's reputation precedes them?"

Liv nodded.

"Well, that phrase was invented for people like your mother, from what I've heard," Renswick said, thoughtfully hanging up her cape and directing her down a long hallway.

The corridor was filled with more black and white paintings of an elfin woman wearing Victorian dresses or horseback riding across a pasture or standing beside a man who looked exactly like Renswick.

"What did my mother's reputation say about her?" Liv dared to ask.

"That she was deadly and ruthless, and absolutely breathtaking in the moonlight," Renswick stated, coming around in front of Liv when he'd led them to an elegant sitting room. He smiled a little. "And that was what her enemies said. Those who liked her said she was brave and just, and incredibly beautiful."

Liv forced herself to look around the sitting room, feeling a tender ache erupt in the pit of her stomach. There was no color. The chairs were black, the marble floors white, and the walls a mixture of both.

"Since the hour is late and you're on duty, do you mind if I offer you nothing?" Renswick asked, motioning for her to take a seat. "I have various bourbons, but I think Warriors prefer to keep their wits about them, is that correct?"

Liv nodded, noticing a decanter stationed by a side window. "I'm fine, Mr. Shoshawnawalla. I won't take up much of your time."

"Please call me Renswick," he offered. "And you passed my tests, so by my own rules, you are welcome to stay as long as you like." He laughed, taking a seat on one of the chairs. "Actually, you're the first to get through my security in a very, very long time. It's been a while since I've had a guest who didn't end up dead."

Liv tried to laugh with him, but it came out more like a sharp cough. "Right, yeah, that was a pretty gnarly security system. Care to explain?"

"I don't like people," Renswick said simply.

"I sensed that, but that was a pretty elaborate system you came up with."

"I just figured that enemies or self-preserving hippies will fight my obstacles," Renswick explained. "But the brave and righteous will persevere using reason. Oh, it is the best gift any of the best possess."

"Your intellect makes sense. I'm just grateful I figured it out before the poltergeist finished me off," Liv stated.

Renswick clapped his hands together with a delighted

grin. "Oh, Todd is simply wonderful, isn't he? He hates people too. At first I didn't need a security system, but then he'd take a holiday, and I'd have to fend for myself. That was when I decided I needed something that was more around the clock."

"Todd?" Liv asked. "That's his name? I think we made a truce."

Renswick chuckled darkly. "Oh, that's cute. I'd hate to be you when you leave here."

"Ummm...can I portal out of here?"

He shook his head. "I'm afraid you can't, but I've got a helmet if you'd like to borrow it. I will require that you return it, which will probably not be worth the effort since you'll need it to get away from Todd the second time."

Liv stared at the ornate coffee table, considering this strange situation. "I think I'm good, but thanks."

"You know what, just this once, I'll call him off of you," Renswick said with a genuine smile. "You appear to have your hands full and you did make it past the gargoyles."

"Thanks," Liv said.

"So, you came here to ask for an exilar? A depour? A trixie mixie?"

Liv's brow scrunched up in confusion. "No, but what's a trixie mixie?"

Renswick wagged a finger at her. "If you don't know, then I can't tell you."

"Right," Liv said, wondering if she'd accidentally strolled into an insane asylum. "I'm here because I've heard you're an expert on demons."

The pleasant smile on Renswick's face disappeared.

"Oh, I should have known." He stood abruptly, clapping his hand at his side. "Please follow me."

The elf disappeared through the sitting room door.

Liv stood and ran after him. "Where are we going?"

"Well, I was under the impression that you were polite company, but I realize that was an incorrect assumption."

"Wait, you thought I came here to ask about tree gnomes and such?" Liv asked, following him up a staircase that seemed to keep going, although she was sure they'd gone up two flights and there were more in sight.

"Naturally," he stated. "Most Warriors who have paid me a visit only care about the trivial."

"And you're surprised I'm asking about demons?" she asked.

He looked over his shoulder, his hand gliding over the staircase rail. "I'm surprised, but not astonished. I figured this day would come soon. Who told you, the dwarves? The centaur? Please tell me the blood children aren't blabbing?"

"It was the brownies," she admitted, wondering what blood children were.

He paused, giving her a proud look. "Brownies? You got the information out of a *brownie*? Oh, Ms. Beaufont, you're doing something right, aren't you?"

"Or something very wrong," she replied.

Renswick halted after five stories, directing her to the only room on the floor. "Please go in, and don't make yourself comfortable."

Liv did as she was told, although she found the tile on this floor sticky, making each step more difficult than the last.

When she entered the open room, she was surprised to find her first bit of color in the house—black, white and too much red. She nearly whipped out Bellator at the sight of the many demons in the room until she realized they were taxidermies.

Liv shivered at the sight before her. It was a library, and so much more. There were many demons complete with horns stationed around the room, as well as many cases displaying different artifacts. With her mouth wide open, she stared around at the strangeness, waiting for Renswick to speak. He seemed to be enjoying her reaction to the room.

"It's taken me the better part of a century to construct this," he offered after a long silence.

"Why?" she asked simply in response.

He shrugged and strode into the room, appreciating the many volumes on the wall. "Why does anyone study the devil?"

"Because they are corrupt?" Liv offered.

He chuckled, holding a single finger in the air. "Or they want to heal the world of corruption."

That sounded similar to what Mortimer had said when she'd asked.

"The crow in the Chamber of the Tree serves a very important purpose," he said.

Liv blinked, wondering how he knew about it. No one but those in the House should know about the crow, and really only the Seven.

"Yes, I know," he said as if she'd voiced a complaint. "You see, most regard the tiger as the most important part because he represents good. But what happens when you ignore evil?"

Liv didn't answer mostly because she didn't have one.

"When you ignore evil, you open yourself to it," he answered for her. Renswick held his arms out wide. "I've spent an entire mortal's life's worth of years cataloging demons because I don't want to be susceptible to them. That's called constant vigilance. That's called guarding the crow, rather than cherishing the tiger."

Liv thought back to the mausoleum, trying to piece together everything she'd learned and seen. "Your wife, Delilah—was she killed by a demon?"

Renswick's arms clapped to his chest, offense springing to his face. "Where is Todd when I need him?"

Liv's hand went to Bellator, but she resisted. Instead, she drew on a strange strength and boldness she hadn't even known she had. "Delilah? Please tell me."

Renswick drew in a breath, collapsing on a long black couch. "You're right. She was bitten by a demon."

Liv didn't know what to say as pain rewrote the elf's face, making him look different than before.

"I constructed this vault of information in an attempt to save her," he explained, motioning to the many volumes in the room.

"And when that didn't save her?" Liv asked, knowing that it hadn't worked.

He chuckled again like this was at all funny. "Then I just continued, believing that maybe one day I could save someone else."

A cold chill ran over her arms. So his wife had died

from a demon's bite. "What happened to her? Did you stop her from becoming one of them?"

He nodded, his eyes distant. "They wonder why I don't play like they do." Renswick indicated to the window at his back that overlooked the park where the hippies congregated. "They don't know what it's like to lop off your wife's head. That's when sanity ends, and the rest begins. I wasn't the same after that. How could I be?"

Liv didn't know what to say. His pain was palpable, and yet, she respected this man more than most she'd met. "But you did it. You stopped your wife from becoming a demon. That was a noble deed, and I'm sure one of her last requests."

He chuckled coldly. "Her last request was to kill me, but I stopped the virus before she was able to complete that mission."

Liv looked at the room around her, realizing exactly what it was now. It was a way to stop the virus. A way to stop demons and keep others from losing their loved ones. Stefan wasn't that for her, but she was still grateful that someone had made this their life's mission.

"Renswick," Liv began carefully. "A demon bit a friend of mine. He's a fellow Warrior. We are trying to control the demon population so that what happened to Delilah doesn't happen to others. Can you help me to find a demon by the name of Sabatore?"

Renswick, who had started to pace, halted. He turned to face Liv, and only then did she realize that his eyes were now black, his pupils mostly hidden. "Did you say Sabatore?"

She gulped. Nodded. "Yes, have you heard of him?"

He closed his eyes, holding his arms out like he was floating. He laughed, but this time it was a loud, a high-pitched sound. "Please tell me this is a joke."

Liv blinked at him. "Wait, no. I'm serious. Do you know of Sabatore?"

He nodded. Opened his eyes. Gave her a stare that communicated a different level of crazy. "Sabatore is the demon who bit Delilah."

CHAPTER FOURTEEN

What were the odds? Liv had been chasing demons for a few weeks, and had been astonished by how many were out there in the world. Renswick's wife and Stefan being bitten by the same demon was like them randomly being related.

"I know it's hard to believe," Renswick said, reading the expression on her face. He looked around at the library. "I've spent quite some time trying to understand demons, and have found that Sabatore is quite different from most. They all have the objective to spread chaos and negativity. When confronted, they will attack a magical creature in defense. However, Sabatore has a vendetta against us. He seeks out magicians and elves, biting them, or 'kissing' them, as the demons like to call it."

"He's intentionally trying to spread the virus?" Liv asked with a gasp.

Renswick nodded. "Yes. He wants to turn as many as possible."

"And that's different from other demons?" Liv asked.

"Most don't care that much about spreading their virus. You see, demons feed off negative emotions, which is why they enjoy creating them in innocent mortals. Sabatore benefits very little by infecting magicians and elves. It's not only a chore for him to search them out since they aren't as widespread as mortals, but it takes him away from the task that would feed him."

"So why does he do it?" Liv asked, although the answer seemed obvious.

Renswick pulled a thick leather-bound book from the shelf. "Sabatore, from everything I've learned, was a magician who was cast out of his tribe. Lost and alone, he searched out demons, begging them to kiss him. When one did, he then went after his family, turning them all. Sabatore has single-handedly spread the virus to more magicians and elves than any other demon."

"So this is his revenge," Liv said with a grimace. "That's sick. How can you want to do that to your own?"

Renswick nodded. He flipped through the book, licking his fingers as he turned the pages. "And what's strangely impressive about him is that he still has much of his personality, and he's still driven by the same motives he was as a magician. My research shows that the demon instinct usually takes over, directing them to the objective of spreading evil. However, that doesn't seem to apply to Sabatore."

"Is that because he was willing to chose the path of a demon?" Liv guessed.

Renswick face brightened with a smile. "Very good, Warrior Beaufont. I'm glad to see you're not all beauty and no brains."

Liv grinned. "I can throw a killer punch too."

He snickered. "Oh, I know you've got strength. I saw you throw your sword at my gargoyle."

She bowed. "Why, thank you."

"And yes, it seems that because Sabatore embraced the demonic ways rather than resisting it like most, he is still in control."

"He fused with the demon instead of having it take over," Liv stated, realizing how strange this situation was. "Stefan couldn't have been bitten by a normal demon. No, he had to get the worst one of all."

Renswick gave her a sympathetic look. "Yes, of all the demons that you could have to take out for your friend's survival, Sabatore is the absolute worst."

"We go big in the House of Seven, and by big, I mean horribly wrong," Liv joked because she couldn't figure out how else to respond to this new information. She couldn't lose hope, but this wasn't what she'd expected to find.

With his head, he indicated the shelves of books. "As you can imagine, Delilah and I researched demons extensively, trying to find out as much about Sabatore as we could, and building this library during the process."

"But in the end, you didn't catch Sabatore in time," Liv supplied.

"That's right," he said somberly. "We were always one step behind him. My sweet wife turned before we got the antidote, and when she finally perished, with her went my desire to kill the demon who took her life."

"But Sabatore is still out there doing to others what he did to Delilah and Stefan," Liv reasoned. "Don't you want to put a stop to him?"

Renswick sighed heavily, defeat on his face. "No, I'm not a brave Warrior like you. I wasn't meant to do the things you do. Delilah and I lived a quiet life here, enjoying the mountain air and our books. When she passed at my hands, I retreated even further, living the life you see now."

Liv looked around at the black, white, and red room. "When she died, you erased the color from your life, didn't you?"

He nodded. "Except in this room, which reminds me never to venture away from home. I know I have many years left to live as an elf, and I've accepted that they will be lonely, but at least I'll be safe."

"So you study demons and document them, but you won't do anything to rid the world of them?" Liv argued, heat burning in her chest suddenly.

To her surprise, Renswick smiled. "Some are meant to study, and some are meant to fight. You, my friend, can't slay Sabatore without me, so I daresay I'm doing my half of the job."

"You know where Sabatore is?" Liv asked in disbelief.

"I didn't when Delilah died. He knew we were tracking him," Renswick explained. "However, since then, I've come upon new leads. Recently, I learned of a demon who met his description. Many mortals reported vampires in this area, and it sounded very much like the activity that happens when Sabatore is kissing magicians and elves."

"Where is he?" Liv asked, craning her head to see the page that Renswick had open.

He tapped his finger on the page. "Louisiana. As of last week, I believe Sabatore is in New Orleans."

Liv didn't allow herself to get excited yet. "Are you sure he's still there?"

He thought for a moment. "It's hard to know for certain, but he usually doesn't move on until he's kissed as many magical creatures as he can find. As you might suspect, there are quite a few in the French Quarter, which is where the activity has been reported."

Liv shivered internally, thinking about how many magicians and elves had fallen victim to Sabatore and were going through the same thing as Stefan. "Thank you. This has been really helpful."

Renswick frowned. "I haven't nearly helped you enough. As I mentioned, I'm a coward who hides in here, expecting you to solve the world's problems with your sword and bravery."

Liv offered a comforting smile. "And like you said, we all have our roles. If he's in New Orleans, you've saved us a lot of time and trouble."

"Once you have Sabatore's blood," Renswick said, shutting the book, "if you bring it here, I'll make the antidote for your friend. I studied the formula at great length, hoping to one day use it on Delilah."

Liv nodded. "Thank you. That would be really helpful. I only wish we had known this and caught him before she died."

Renswick laid the book on an end table, looking around. "I regret her death more than anything in this world, but I've come to accept it. Maybe if you stop Sabatore, I'll finally get the closure I've been longing for."

That gave Liv hope that there was still a way to save the

man before her. Maybe more than just Stefan could benefit from slaying Sabatore.

"Renswick, my friend is not looking well. He says it's getting harder to control the demon's voice in him, and his energy is waning." Liv drew in a breath, surprised by the regret in her voice. "How much longer do you think he has?"

Renswick motioned to the door, ushering Liv out. "It's hard to say. However, I've learned that fighting the demon inside the person is incredibly difficult and painful. The moment that my sweet Delilah turned was the very same that she quit fighting. Don't get me wrong—she was tough, tougher than most, but even the strongest can only fight for so long. When your friend decides he doesn't want to deal with the demon anymore, that's when he'll turn, and there will be no saving him."

CHAPTER FIFTEEN

Stefan was crouched against the brick wall in the alley, appearing more like a homeless drug addict than a Warrior for the House of Seven.

Liv approached him carefully, her hand on Bellator. She couldn't see his face and didn't know if it was still him or if he'd in fact turned. Renswick's words were still fresh in her mind, infecting every second with dread. She couldn't imagine doing what he'd done—swinging his sword's blade across his wife's neck. She couldn't blame him for being a recluse now. That man had more demons in his closet than most. She didn't laugh at the horrible pun.

"Stefan?" she asked, keeping a safe distance from him as raspy breaths emerged from his mouth.

When he looked up where his head was resting on his forearms, the morning light shone on his pale skin. He was still him, but only barely.

"I don't think I can take anymore," he said through cracked lips.

Liv shook her head at him, taking her hand off Bellator

and pulling him to his feet. "Yes, you can, because you're Stefan-freaking-Ludwig. You're a demon hunter and have many more to kill, but only once we take out Sabatore."

His body sagged under her arm. "Liv, it's too hard. I'm so tired, and it's useless. No one ever catches the demon who bit them. It's futile."

Liv gripped him with a fierceness that surprised even her. Stefan's eyes widened from the act, and he stood up straight. She couldn't tell him that the moment he gave up would be his last. Stefan already knew that on some level, she believed. Surrendering to the demon would be a relief, and she could tell by the look in his eyes that he was exhausted and tired of fighting.

"You know what? No one ever catches the demon who bit them, but those people also aren't you," she began. "You're the one who opposes the council, showing mercy to unregistered magicians. Your grandparents freed an entire village of magical creatures who were slaves to magicians. You're a champion, and this isn't going to be Stefan Ludwig's end. This is only part of your story. One day we're going to laugh about this, but first, we have to go and slay Sabatore."

Stefan looked to be having trouble swallowing as he took in her words. "Yeah, let's get right on that. But first, we have to know where to look. Did you get any leads?"

"If by leads, you mean do I know exactly where we need to search, then yes," Liv said, opening a portal to the French Quarter.

"No. Just no, Liv," Stefan argued as they clung to the shadows in an alley similar to the one they had left, but this one was in New Orleans.

"It's a good plan," she said. He'd perked up when she had told him where Sabatore was, but then slumped again when she described the plan.

"It's too dangerous," Stefan stated.

"And yet, it's a brilliant plan that you can't argue with."

"I won't allow it."

"Then I'll do it on my own," she said. "I am supposed to be hunting demons, and he sounds like the mother of them all to end."

Stefan laughed coldly. "It makes sense that he's the one spreading the virus so rapidly."

"Okay, then it's settled." Liv strode into the morning sunlight, away from the bustling thoroughfare where tourists were strolling towards a less trafficked lane

Stefan reached for her, but she was too fast. "Liv, don't do this."

She turned, walking backward. "I *am* doing this, and the only person who can save me is you. So don't freaking give up, Stefan."

He gave her a look that could have killed her. "Please," he pleaded. "Please don't do this."

Liv halted. "If it were me in your position, what would *you* do?"

He bit his bottom lip. "I'd play on what we know about Sabatore, using it to our advantage so that we drew him out and finished him off. Then I'd help you save yourself, hoping that one day you'd thank me for my courageous deeds but not expecting you to. Simply pining for that possibility."

"It's gone to your head," she joked. "You're starting to hallucinate by reciting bad poetry."

"And in this fantasy where you thank me, you'd be wearing a cotton sundress," he continued.

"Yes, it might be too late to save you," she remarked. "You've gone completely insane."

Stefan managed to crack a sideways smile at her. "I think you'd look good in yellow daisies."

"When did everyone start vocally disapproving of the way I dress?" Liv asked.

"We've always talked about it behind your back, but recently decided to start an intervention."

Liv shook her head. "There are much bigger problems in the world."

"Yes, like the fact that the best Warrior the House of Seven has is about to make herself bait for the most vicious demon in this world," Stefan shot back bitterly.

Liv flashed him a rebellious smile. "I don't know about that Warrior bit, but yes to being bait, so don't let me get kissed, Stefan. Save my ass before it's too late." She spun around, hurrying for the abandoned passage on the other side the buildings. *And let's hope we save your ass as well before it's too late,* she thought, feeling a cold wind sweep over her cheeks as she exited into an empty courtyard.

CHAPTER SIXTEEN

J ust *act casual,* Liv told herself as she strolled through the deserted passage. The sound of jazz and the smell of fried food were strong in the air, a deceptive combination that sought to erase the stark reality of the situation. This wasn't a vacation in the French Quarter. This was a death mission that would result in either the death of a demon or Stefan Ludwig. And if things went completely to hell, it would be Liv's end too. However, she tried to not think of that.

She considered whistling like she didn't have a care in the world, but that just seemed silly. When she got to the section of the avenue where Sabatore had attacked several magicians and elves, according to Renswick, Liv pretended to be lost.

She paused, looking around as if she were trying to get her bearings. Bellator rested on her hip under her cape, but she would only pull it if she absolutely had to. Hopefully, it wouldn't come to that. Stefan needed to rescue her. She'd considered slaughtering Sabatore on her own, but this had to be Stefan's kill. That demon had put him through hell, and he deserved to be the one who finished him for good, ridding the world of his unique brand of evil.

Liv only hoped that Stefan could do it. That he was strong enough. That he was up for the challenge. Everything was riding on her faith in him.

Taking a deep breath, Liv looked up, trying to appear as though she didn't know which way to go, like there was a giant compass painted in the sky. The lost were easy targets. The more lost she appeared, the less Sabatore would be expecting the ass-kicking that followed.

Maybe if she wasn't expecting it, Liv wouldn't have heard the footsteps on the catwalk overhead on the building behind her. Before she'd started hunting demons, she'd never expected to find them strolling around in broad daylight. Since then, she had learned that they preferred the light, when the lost and lonely were least expecting them. People were on guard at night, fearful of what lurked in the shadows, but in the daylight, most had their guard down.

The sound of two feet landing on the bricks of the alley didn't make Liv tense. She'd expected it; expected the grand entrance. Again, it was so quiet that if she hadn't been anticipating it, she wouldn't have noticed the demon landing at her back or the swish of his jacket as he stood.

She refrained from moving her hand to Bellator. Not defending herself was against her very instincts—and the thing she did next was also.

Liv slapped her hand to her head, appearing to be completely stumped by her complex predicament. "Oh, you dumb blonde. How could you have gotten yourself lost once again," she said, talking to herself.

The smell of a disgusting demon wafted to her nostrils, replacing the other, better odors in the corridor. Most didn't know what a demon smelled like, not even magicians. That was because when one met a demon, one didn't survive the encounter. One merely thought that the smell was the sewage in the underground or a dead animal rotting nearby. However, Liv had been trained by one of the best demon hunters alive, and she knew that smell well; it meant that death was coming close. But not for her. Not that day.

The hands that reached around her, pinning her arms to her side, were the strongest she'd ever felt. Looking down, she saw the slick red skin, a telltale sign of a demon. "Time to die, blondie," a voice that was reminiscent of her worst nightmares whispered in her ear. Those awful dreams seemed to play in fast forward in her head, filling her with every horrible emotion they'd ever given her.

She pretended to struggle, using half her strength. However, she'd need all her power to fight this demon. Liv dropped to the ground, trying to pull Sabatore over her head. He laughed in her ear, holding her upright. He was very strong. If Stefan didn't come through, she was absolutely screwed.

Sabatore hugged her to his chest, nearly crushing her, then grabbed her hand, spinning her out like they were doing a strange dance.

And then she saw him. Liv had seen dozens of demons in the last several weeks. However, in all her life, she'd never seen anything as revolting as the beast that stood before her.

Two spiral horns sprouted from his bald red head, and his black eyes blinked at her with a sinister heat she'd never before encountered. Scars marked his face, long streaks that ran over his chin and along his cheekbones, the results of his many brutal battles. And when Sabatore's nostrils flared, he also bared a row of sharp, pointy teeth.

"You are one ugly mudder," she said, trying to yank her hand from his grasp but unable to.

"And you'll look as awful as me one day, magician," he said, forcing her to twirl around like he was leading her on the dance floor.

If she was going to fight him, she'd use her other hand to pull Bellator right then, but that wasn't the plan. She kind of doubted it would work anyway. Something told her that Sabatore knew she was carrying a weapon, and she wouldn't draw it from its sheath before he knocked it from her hands.

Sabatore yanked Liv into him, making it impossible to ignore the rancid smell radiating off him. She was forced to lay a hand to his chest to try to stop the momentum. His hot breath drifted down on her cheeks, nearly making her vomit.

"I'm going to enjoy this more than usual," he said with a growl, a morbid smile on his face.

Liv pretended to resist. "Let me go."

His laugh sounded like gravel underfoot. "Oh, no. You're a noble magician. I'd love nothing more than ridding this Earth of you."

Liv tried to push him back and he simply tightened his grip on her, seemingly amused by her attempts.

"Pucker up, love," he said, pulling her close, his mouth inches from her neck as he leaned down to her.

Liv pressed her eyes closed, praying that Stefan would come through. Hoping her faith in him hadn't been misplaced.

Sabatore's mouth came unhinged, his razor-sharp teeth a stark contrast against his blood-red skin. He lowered his head farther, about to deliver what he'd promised and done to so many magicians and elves—turning magic into pure evil, blotting it from this Earth. Turning magical creatures into the destruction of mankind.

The monster purred, as if this was an act that brought him ultimate satisfaction. Liv's pulse quickened, and she held her breath. Tensed all over, and uttered a last-minute prayer—her final wish: *Please don't let me die. I can't abandon Sophia. I can't let Clark down. Familia est sempiternum.*

She squeezed her eyes shut.

CHAPTER SEVENTEEN

L iv's feet came off the ground. She thought that Sabatore had picked her up, but then he let out a guttural scream. Craning her neck, she realized something had lifted him too.

He released her, dropping her to the brick pavement rather ungracefully. She turned over at once and started crab-walking backward on her hands and feet. What she saw next almost didn't register at first.

Stefan picked Sabatore up by the back of his coat and launched him into the air, throwing him halfway across the courtyard.

The man she'd come to know the last few weeks as a friend had a red face, and his blue eyes had gone dark. She blinked, hoping that what she thought she was seeing was wrong. For the first time ever, he looked more like a demon than himself, and the growl that escaped his mouth sounded exactly like that of a demon on a rampage.

Sabatore jumped to his feet, letting out a similar-sounding growl. The two faced off, staring at each other with a heat that spoke of their personal vendetta.

Liv backed up, her hand on Bellator. She'd been preparing herself mentally to take Stefan down if the need should arise, but she hadn't considered that she might have to defeat him and Sabatore on the same day. However, it appeared that Stefan was close to turning. How much longer did he have?

His eyes darted to her with a frustrated growl. He didn't look at her as he had before. His gaze was murderous now. Hungry.

"Stefan?" she asked in a whisper. "Are you okay?"

He nodded. "I will be. Don't worry, I know what I'm doing."

Don't worry? She was trapped in a courtyard with a demon and soon-to-be demon. Worry was all she could do.

Stefan's heated gaze turned back on the demon on the other side of the courtyard, who was starting to prowl back and forth, his long coat billowing around him.

"So one of my children has found me," Sabatore began. "And right before he turns, too. You think you have time, but if your strength and speed have increased, it's too late."

Stefan ground his teeth together, his eyes narrowing to slits. "I have time."

Sabatore laughed, his voice echoing around the courtyard and disrupting a flock of birds high on the roof of the two-story home beside them. "You have less time than you think. You'll turn, and then you'll kill your first magician as a demon, keeping this beautiful cycle going." He indicated Liv, who had her hand around Bellator's hilt. She couldn't allow Stefan to turn. More than anything, she wanted to take Sabatore out right then, ending this.

However, she reminded herself that this wasn't her fight. This was Stefan's kill.

Although she was battling internally, she couldn't argue that Stefan looked close to his end. Before what could have been seen as a flush of his skin was definitely the mark of demonism. His face was unnaturally red, and his eyes were almost black. His speed was incredible as he sprinted across the courtyard, picking Sabatore up by the collar and holding him high above his head.

"I'm in control," Stefan stated. " And I'm not giving in to the demon."

Sabatore laughed again. "You can't keep it at bay forever. You've already turned. You have the demon's powers, and soon the rest of you will join it. That's the only way to end the burning inferno inside you."

"I won't!" Stefan yelled, throwing Sabatore across the courtyard into the brick wall. It cracked, showering broken pieces down on him.

The demon pushed up, shaking his head with a cold chuckle.

"I like your spirit," Sabatore remarked. "I was right to turn you. You'll make a fine demon."

"That will never happen," Stefan replied, charging Sabatore and thrusting his fist at his head. The demon caught it, spinning his fist around and knocking Stefan to the pavement, his arm curved unnaturally behind his back as the demon took the advantage.

Standing over him, Sabatore grimaced. "In all my years, none of my children have ever tracked me down. This is a first. You are a worthy opponent, but your day is done. It's time to turn."

"No!" Stefan said, his face marked by pain as Sabatore continued to twist his arm until he dislocated his shoulder.

"Do as I say and it will be better," Sabatore commanded. "The pain will be gone. Your days will be easy. All you have to do is give in."

Stefan jerked away, being released. "No. You're a monster. I'm not you. I never will be."

Liv watched from the sidelines, unsure if they knew she was still there. She couldn't leave, and yet intervening felt wrong since Stefan still seemed to be in control. But for how long?

"I'm the only thing pure in this world," Sabatore said, striding over to Stefan, who was trying to work his shoulder back into place as painful screams ripped from his mouth. "Demons are the only creatures that make sense. Our purpose is clear. We are not corrupted by love or blasphemy. By rejection or fear. We give that which we are. We are the essence of this world. Evil is the only way. All good is actually evil. Very soon you'll see that."

With a crack, Stefan yanked his shoulder back into place, rolling it out, along with his neck. "I am Stefan Ludwig. I'm a demon hunter. A magician. A Warrior. My job is to rid the world of evil, and that starts with you."

He threw his fist at Sabatore and this time it connected, knocking him back against the same brick wall, making more of it crumble.

The demon laughed as he pushed up, undeterred. "You know nothing of this world."

In a movement that Liv's eyes didn't register

completely, the demon sprang to his feet, staying low, his leg coming around and knocking Stefan to the ground. He stomped on his stomach, making him convulse. An anguished moan fell from his mouth.

"Oh, yes. It won't be long," Sabatore said. "You'll join me soon. And before then, I'll ensure that your magician friend is ready for you. She'll be your first, and that's always the best."

With Stefan still in pain, Sabatore sped over to Liv, arriving in front of her faster than she would have anticipated.

"You were going to be mine," he said, roughly pushing her hair out of her face. "But this will be better."

She felt Bellator pulse in her hand. It knew what needed to be done. It was begging her to do it. However, her instinct still told her that this had to be Stefan's kill. She believed in him.

Stefan ran at the demon, jumping and flying through the air. Landing straight behind Sabatore, he yanked him off of Liv, throwing him once more through the air.

The demon skidded across the bricks, slamming into a wrought iron patio chair and table. Stefan sprang into the air again, landing beside Sabatore. He picked the chair up and slammed it across his back as he tried to get up. The demon crumpled to the ground. Stefan was about to swing the chair again when Sabatore grabbed his leg, yanking it out from under him. Stefan fell, landing beside him. The demon crawled on top of him, about to throw a punch, when Stefan took his momentum, rolling over and springing up.

The two moved so quickly that Liv had trouble telling

exactly what they were doing to each other. She saw several punches exchanged, and black blood sprinkled the pavement. She didn't know if now was the time that she should intervene. Liv wanted to do something but she didn't know how to help Stefan without potentially harming him. What she did know was that this fight would be over soon, and the danger would only be beginning for her. Whether it was Stefan or Sabatore who won, she'd have a demon to deal with.

Sabatore had risen to his feet, hauling Stefan up with him. As if returning the favor from before, he threw him at the crumbling brick wall. Stefan nearly went through it. He landed on the ground in a crumpled heap.

Oh, this isn't good, Liv thought, pulling Bellator out.

Standing over Stefan, Sabatore spat on him before yanking the Warrior's sword from its sheath and throwing it across the courtyard.

"You're ungrateful," Sabatore said in a coarse whisper. "I saved you, and this is how you thank me? I will make you see the error of your ways." He picked Stefan up by the neck, hauling him to his feet. "You'll start by kissing the magician. Then you'll know I was right and will turn completely."

Stefan tried to claw Sabatore, but his attempts did not make contact with the demon, although they made him laugh.

Liv tensed when Sabatore dragged Stefan over to her, blood trickling from his nose and mouth.

"Do it or I will," Sabatore ordered.

Stefan jerked his head back and forth. For as much as he looked like a demon now, he was still him. Liv knew it.

Taking his hands off Stefan, Sabatore pushed him in her direction.

"If *I* do it, I'll kill her," Sabatore said. "You can't win against me. Kiss her, and it will be done."

Stefan's lips were quivering as he stumbled in Liv's direction. He was now only three feet away.

She prepared to swing Bellator, but part of her knew she wouldn't be fast enough, not to defeat Stefan nor Sabatore. They were too strong, like super-demons. Stefan must have inherited it from Sabatore. And when he turned, he'd be even stronger. Even worse.

"I'm sorry," Stefan said, regret in his eyes. Liv made an attempt, holding Bellator firmly. In a blur, Stefan blocked her, knocking the sword out of her hands, and grabbing it by the hilt with his free hand.

Liv tensed and backed up as he swung the sword around and lopped off Sabatore's head. It flew several feet, rolling until he was staring at them with his black eyes.

Stefan pulled out his handkerchief, wiping the black blood from the blade.

With a beautiful grace, he turned to Liv, handing her the sword. "I'm sorry I used your sword. I hope you don't mind."

CHAPTER EIGHTEEN

"**A**re you okay?" Liv asked Stefan for what felt like the hundredth time as they strode up to Renswick's house. She really hoped she didn't have to pass the gargoyles' test again.

He nodded, his demon eyes giving her a look that she couldn't interrupt.

He'd taken Sabatore's blood without a word before hurrying behind her through the portal to Renswick's house.

She wished he had said something in response to her question instead of simply nodding.

Once they stepped across the threshold of the yard, a small boulder raced through the air at them. Liv held up her hand, blowing it to pieces.

"Seriously, Todd, not right now," Liv said to the poltergeist. "I know I said I'd play with you later, but I'm super busy trying to save this man from becoming a demon."

Liv looked back at Stefan, but he didn't appear amused.

Instead, he pointed at the house. "This is where the elf who can help lives?"

That was the first time he'd said anything since apologizing to her for using her sword to kill Sabatore. Now she understood why he didn't speak. He sounded different. His voice was more demonic.

"Yes, Renswick promised to help," she said, hurrying up the stairs, the gargoyles staying still on the roof.

Liv knocked the giant metal claw on the front of the door. The seconds that passed felt like the longest ones ever. For a moment, she wondered if Renswick had actually gone out for once. That would be the worst timing.

Her fear dissipated when he opened the door, his face neutral and then quickly shifting to fear at the sight of Stefan.

"He's not a demon yet," she said in response to his bulging eyes.

"He's entirely too close," Renswick said, waving them into the house.

"I'm fine," Stefan argued. "I'm in control."

Liv believed him, but she knew that for Renswick it was like reliving a nightmare. Had Delilah held on like this, finally giving up when the pain was too much? Liv couldn't even imagine the internal agony Stefan was experiencing. It must have been like trying to stay awake when every part of her body was begging for sleep. It was like resisting eating when starving and a feast lay before her. It was depriving oneself of relief when a simple choice would make it all better.

"Did you do it?" Renswick asked, looking her over.

She pointed at Stefan. "He did it."

Renswick exhaled loudly. "Sabatore is gone?"

Stefan pulled the vial of blood from his cape, handing it to Renswick. They'd taken it from Sabatore's body using the vial that Renswick had given her. "He can no longer spread his disease to the innocent."

"I never thought I'd see the day," Renswick said, grabbing the vial.

"I actually didn't either," Stefan said through clenched teeth, the very act of speaking appearing as if it was too much for him. "I wouldn't have been able to do it if it hadn't been for this one here." He nodded in Liv's direction.

Renswick ran his thumb affectionately over the vial of black blood. "We all should have a Liv Beaufont in our life."

Liv shook her head. "I did nothing."

"You didn't give up, which is why I'm holding on now," Stefan said.

"Take him up to the first bedroom on your right," Renswick ordered, directing her up the stairs. "I'll be up with the antidote in a minute. I have it all ready to go. All I have to do is add this."

Once they were in the room, Liv pointed to the bed, but Stefan didn't move. He simply stared at her with a strange craze in his black eyes. "I'm sorry that you have to see me this way."

She backed out of the bedroom, the smell wafting off him finally hitting her in the nose. He was changing. Even more.

"It's fine," she lied.

He shook his head. "No, it's not. My only hope is that you'll forget this when it's over."

"It's hard to forget when the ones we love become our worst nightmare," Renswick said at their back, having appeared soundlessly. "But more importantly, why would you ever want someone to forget the strength you've shown battling this? You are a stronger man than most, Stefan Ludwig."

He handed the vial to Stefan. "Drink that lying down. And I'm sorry to tell you, but whatever pain you're experiencing right now might get worse."

"Might?" Liv asked.

"Someone being healed of demonism is almost unheard of," Renswick explained. "The documentation I've read said that it hurts like hell."

Stefan drank the antidote in one swift movement. "I'll take hell over eternal damnation any day."

"He will never be the same," Renswick explained to Liv as she paced in front of the open window in the sitting room. Outside the yard was full of color, unlike in the house, where black and white and various grays monopolized her vision.

"Will he look like a demon?" Liv asked.

Renswick poured her a glass of bourbon. "No, that will be gone within the hour. However, in nearly fusing with the demon, he's become well acquainted with evil."

Liv spun abruptly. "Will he be bad now?"

Renswick shook his head. "Quite the opposite. He's going to be repulsed by evil. Most likely he will have an allergic reaction when in contact with evil. However, like I said, this is not well documented since it is a rare case, so Stefan will defy the odds."

"He fights demons," Liv stated. "I don't think it will be a problem for him to have an allergic reaction to evil."

Renswick poured himself a glass as well. "Before, he went after that which he was assigned. He will now hate evil so thoroughly that it will always feel like a personal vendetta."

"Why is that a bad thing?" Liv asked, wondering if she was missing something.

"It may not be," Renswick said. "However, please remember that this world is not balanced without good and bad. As much as I hate to admit it, evil serves a purpose. If we wiped it out completely, our planet would be full of gray. It is evil that gives color to good. Evil highlights the holy power of goodness."

"So what am I supposed to do?" Liv asked, feeling somehow responsible for Stefan now.

"You may not be able to do anything," Renswick said, taking a sip of his bourbon. "But you might be able to ensure that he doesn't lose his mind trying to stomp out all evil in the world. That agenda would end the best of men. It is an impossible job."

CHAPTER NINETEEN

L iv could hardly believe how normal Stefan looked as he stood in front of the Door of Reflection. His color was back, and his blue eyes sparkled with a new intensity. There was no sign that he'd been bitten by a demon except for the scar on his forearm.

He pulled his sleeve down, covering it, giving her a proud look. "You're staring."

She shook her head, trying to dispel her disbelief. "It's just that it hasn't been that long, and you look so...so..."

"Normal?" he said, finishing her sentence.

"No, that's not what I was thinking," she replied. She didn't know how to say that Stefan Ludwig looked better than normal. There was a new confidence in his eyes. Several times as they traveled back from Renswick's, she'd seen him blur as he moved. Liv suspected that he retained the super strength too. Multiple times she had to stop herself from asking him about it. She didn't know if Stefan wanted to be reminded that he was still part demon and would be for the rest of his long life, which Renswick thought might be longer than most magicians. He was the best part of the demon, and yet he was only a magician again. It defied reason and made Stefan one of the most unique magicians in the world. And no one could know about it. That had been the one thing he'd requested as they entered the House of Seven minutes prior.

"Please keep my secret," he had said as they strode through the long hallway covered in the ancient language.

"Of course," Liv had replied. Now, staring at him, she wanted to say so much, ask him so many questions. He didn't look deterred by the way she continuously ran her eyes over his face.

"Are you ready to report?" Stefan asked, gesturing at the Door of Reflection.

Liv released a small, proud smile. "Oh, I freaking can't wait for this."

Stefan returned the grin. "Yes, and I look forward to seeing the relief on Hester's face."

Liv took a step toward the Door of Reflection, pulling her eyes away from Stefan.

"Oh, and Liv?" he said at her back, making her turn.

"Yes?" she replied.

"I owe you my life," he told her simply.

She shook her head. "No, you owe me nothing. Friends save each other. I only did the same thing you'd do for me."

He took a step closer to her, his eyes dancing with a strange intensity. "I've never had a friend like you; someone who would risk their life for mine."

"That's because you usually have blood splattered on your boots, which most who would like to be your friend would find really gross," Liv said with a laugh.

A smile lit his eyes. "And you're right. If it had been you, I'd have risked everything to save you. But the thing I love about you is that you don't need to be saved. You, Liv Beaufont, are unlike anyone I've ever met."

Liv didn't know what to say. She was hyper-aware of how close Stefan was to her. Of the racing of her heart, and the way her breathing was suddenly shallow.

Maybe sensing her nervousness, he took a step back and pointed at the Door of Reflection. "I think that we're officially 'Liv Beaufont' late. That should set the right tone for this meeting with the council."

Liv laughed. "That's my style." A second time, she started for the Door of Reflection.

"Oh, and one more thing," Stefan said when she was only a couple of feet from the door. Liv was about to turn, but before she could, Stefan raced around her, taking the spot right in front of the door. "In case you're wondering, I did keep the speed and strength of the demon."

Liv gulped. He was even closer than before. "I *was* wondering."

He nodded. "I know. I can sort of read you."

"Is that another benefit of almost becoming a demon?" Liv asked.

Stefan grinned. "No, that just applies to you."

The council was quiet when Liv took her spot next to Stefan in the Chamber of the Tree. They appeared to be busy reviewing their devices. Since they were the only two

Warriors in attendance, she had thought they'd receive the council's immediate attention.

"You're late," Adler said, not looking up.

"We were busy slaying demons," Liv answered.

Hester glanced up, surprise springing to her face. "You're both here!"

Stefan smiled, his hands clasped behind his back as he rose a couple of inches. "I missed you all and decided to pay the council a visit."

She winked at him with joy in her eyes. "I missed you too, Warrior Ludwig."

Adler sighed, annoyance heavy on his face. "Really, showing such sentiments is highly unprofessional. You both know that."

Liv gave Stefan a sideways look. "Remember that we're not humans with emotions. We're robots."

He nodded. "Copy that, Robot Beaufont."

Adler rolled his eyes, finally looking up. "The council is extremely busy reviewing a developing case. Go ahead and make your report, and make it fast."

"In addition to slaying over two dozen demons, we've put an end to a demon responsible for heavily spreading the disease," Stefan stated.

Clark glanced up then, his attention piqued.

"Mr. Ludwig, inflating your numbers will do you no favors," Adler said.

Liv looked at Stefan. "He's right. That number is way off."

Stefan agreed with a nod. "Yes, I totally forgot about that nest in Texas. It was actually three dozen."

"That's incredible," Raina said, giving them a wide

smile. "Great job, you two."

"Yes, it appears that you two make a good team," Hester stated.

Stefan grinned at Liv. "Yes, we have a nice dynamic."

"Did I hear you right?" Haro asked. "Did you slay the one they call the Master Demon?"

Stefan pushed his jacket back, resting his hand on his sword. "Yes, Sabatore is gone."

There was muttering from the council.

"Sabatore?" Lorenzo said, a question in his tone. "I didn't know demons had names."

"They were once people," Liv stated at once. "We should never forget that."

"If you have in fact slain the Master Demon, that will significantly affect the demon population," Bianca said.

"We did in fact slay him," Liv corrected. "I dropped his head off in your room. I thought you might want it."

"You did not!" Bianca yelled, her nostrils flaring.

"Oh, you didn't want it?" Liv asked before glancing at Stefan. "I probably shouldn't have put it in her bed."

"Ms. Beaufont, that is quite enough," Adler spat.

"Oh, did *you* want the head?" Liv asked, not at all deterred by his tone.

"I think we all know that no one here wants a demon's severed head," Adler stated.

"Actually, proof that the Master Demon is dead would be quite valuable," Haro corrected. "That's a feat that will gain much favor from the magical community, as well as create a great deal of good will with the elves. This is the key we were looking for with the current negotiations."

Adler threw his arm in Stefan and Liv's direction. "Do you see either of them carrying a demon's head?"

"The giant horns on the top of Sabatore's head wouldn't fit in the duffle bag I had. That was why we took a picture and filed it with our report," Liv stated.

All of the Councilors' head turned down as they began reviewing the files.

"Wow, you killed this beast?" Clark, the first to glance up, asked.

Liv pointed at Stefan. "He did it, actually."

Stefan smiled. "It was one hundred percent a team effort. I couldn't have done it without her."

Adler didn't look impressed when he looked up. "Again, your comradery has no place in these meetings."

"I think it absolutely does," Hester argued.

"Ms. DeVries, we have more pressing matters than hearing these two exchange kudos," Adler stated.

"Although we are quite busy," Raina began, "these Warriors have achieved an incredible thing and should be able to celebrate. Actually, I think they deserve to be rewarded."

Adler sighed again, one of his favorite things to do. "A Warrior doesn't get rewards for doing their job."

"Maybe that's something we should change," Clark interjected, displaying new confidence against Adler.

"We aren't in the position to make changes to our processes at the moment," Bianca said. "We're in the middle of a huge negotiation."

"Which, as we just discussed, might go much smoother now," Haro said.

"Enough," Adler said, slamming his fist on the bench. "Ms. Beaufont, have you gone to visit the giants yet?"

"Nope," Liv said casually. "I've been busy ridding the world of demons."

"But it was you who said you could do both cases," Adler argued.

"And I plan to," Liv stated.

"Then make it happen," Adler said. "And Mr. Ludwig, hopefully, you can still get rid of demons without Ms. Beaufont holding your hand?"

"What? We're being split up?" Stefan asked, the smile dropping from his face.

"Well, yes," Adler said, browsing his device, suddenly appearing distracted. "Ms. Beaufont made another commitment to the council, and since you two have reduced the demon population again, I see no reason why two Warriors should be assigned to the case. Does everyone else agree?"

There was a collective murmuring of yeses from the council.

"Very well, then," Adler stated dismissively. "Ms. Beaufont, we'll expect a prompt report from you regarding the giants' response."

Liv was about to make a smartass remark to that when the black crow landed in the middle of the floor and stared at Stefan.

His hand jerked to his sword, pulling it in a flash. All of the Councilors looked up at the sound of the blade being whipped out of its sheath.

Their eyes darted to Stefan, who was regarding the crow with brooding contempt, and then to the bird.

"Mr. Ludwig, what are you doing?" Adler asked.

"He's simply showing everyone the sword that was used to slay Sabatore," Liv lied, since it was Bellator that had killed the master demon.

Adler nodded slowly, disbelief in his gaze. "That's not necessary, and I believe you've both been dismissed."

"Right," Liv agreed, grabbing Stefan's arm and yanking him toward the Door of Reflection. "Come on, let's leave the council to do their thing."

Stefan followed her reluctantly at first, his eyes staying trained on the crow as if he were resisting a strong urge to slaughter it. This was what Renswick had meant: Stefan would forever feel a unique brand of hate toward evil. And she'd do as Renswick had advised and help him so that it didn't overpower him and make him irrational.

CHAPTER TWENTY

Sophia wasn't quite finished with the disguising spell that would make Liv look like Decar Sinclair. She could hardly believe that the child magician could master such a complex spell, and yet if anyone could do it, it would be the girl who was an expert at hiding.

This break gave Liv some much-needed time to study Bermuda's book and train. She felt she could spend the next several hundred years studying magic and barely scratch the surface; that was how vast and complicated it was. Her father had called it the "endless artform."

"You're starting to rely more on instinct," Akio said after they finished sparring that afternoon. "Before you thought about your next move, but now you're allowing Bellator to lead you more."

As Liv toweled off in the training studio, she told Akio about how Bellator had acted like a guide when she'd been hunting demons.

He nodded, not at all surprised. "Warrior Ludwig is

correct. Your sword *is* more than a weapon. If you treat it as a valuable friend, that is what it will become."

"It's funny that you both talk about swords like they are living beings," Liv remarked, studying Bellator. It didn't look any different after being used to slay Sabatore, but for some reason, it felt different.

With a serious expression, Akio said, "The difference between a good Warrior and a great one is the latter sees their weapon as having a pulse and a spirit. A good Warrior uses it as a tool, but your sword was created with a timeless magic. There is no other tool like that in the world, I can assure you of that."

"So do you think that the skill Bellator offers me is about being my guide?" Liv asked, having thought about this at length lately. Turbinger's mark was eventually lethal, and it stored every memory from every battle within it. Rory had said that the extra benefit a giant-made sword offered its bearer was unique and only surfaced when that person bonded properly with it.

"I think that could be one of the benefits," Akio mused, running his studious eyes over the blade. "However, like any friend, the sword can offer different advantages depending on the situation." He withdrew his own sword, which was curved, its hilt made of minotaur bones.

"Once when I was in battle, Rakurai illuminated my path in very much the same way your sword did for you recently," Akio explained, referring to his own weapon, which his great-grandfather had named when he'd forged the blade for the grandson who would one day become a Warrior for the House of Seven.

"However, if I went into every battle expecting that of

Rakurai, I might become too dependent on it and not use my own skills," Akio stated. "It's important to keep an open mind so that you don't limit yourself or Bellator."

This was fascinating to Liv. She hadn't realized there was so much magic around weapons. They were alive, and that made her even prouder to be a Warrior. "What other benefits has Rakurai offered you?"

A slight smile wisped to Akio's face. "It has guided me when I was lost, healed me when I was wounded, and directed my hand in battle. However, much like a relationship with a lover, some of the intimate details should remain private. That's part of forming the bond that will furnish you with further benefits."

"So, is Bellator supposed to be my friend or my lover?" Liv asked, growing confused, but that was typical when talking to Akio. He liked to talk in riddles, which she found somewhat entertaining.

"Shouldn't every lover be your friend first?" Akio asked.

Liv nodded. "Yes, I guess people need to like each other before they love each other."

Akio nodded.

Liv regarded Bellator with amusement. "I guess I should take you to dinner, then. Something with candlelight."

Akio's eyes flicked to the door as he straightened.

Liv turned to find his older brother standing in the doorway. Haro was watching them curiously.

"Do you need something from me, brother?" Akio asked.

Haro shook his head. "Unless you'd like to accompany us," he said, motioning between Liv and him. "I was hoping that Warrior Beaufont would join me in my study for a drink."

Liv tilted her head to the side, not expecting this invitation. She glanced at Akio with a question in her eyes.

"We are done training for today," Akio said, seemingly dismissing her. "And I should devote the rest of my attention to my case, but thank you for the offer, brother."

"Very well," Haro said. "Warrior Beaufont, are you free to join me? I think it's overdue that we speak."

Liv didn't know what that meant. She didn't think she was supposed to be spending one-on-one time with Councilors, although there was nothing that strictly forbade it. She just didn't know what Haro would want to talk to her about.

Intrigued, she strode in his direction. "Sure. I could use a drink after taking that beating."

"You took it better than the last time," Akio said with a laugh in his voice.

"Thank you...I think." Liv waved as she followed Haro out. He was silent as he strode urgently down the hallway, his silk robes billowing out behind him. He looked almost exactly like his brother, although he was much older. Akio, she'd noticed, treated him more like a father figure than a brother. Maybe that was a part of their culture, or maybe it was due to the age difference.

When they'd come to the Takahashi residence, Haro held the door open for Liv. Their living space was very different from the suite where Clark and Sophia lived. Her siblings' place was warm, with oil paintings and musical instruments. The furniture was reminiscent of old English design. In contrast, the Takahashi home had low tables and sitting areas. Decorative partitions sectioned off the main living room. Liv felt as though she had stepped through a portal into Tokyo.

"My study is through there," Haro stated, indicating a door. "I thought that would be a nice place for us to talk, but if you prefer a more neutral territory, we can go to the main dining area. It's just that it offers little privacy, and I prefer the sake I keep on hand rather than what the chef stocks."

"This is fine," Liv said, still unsure what Haro could possibly want to talk to her about. Why would they need privacy.

The study was similar in design to the main living area. It was rich with books and beautiful Japanese artwork.

When Haro indicated a seat, Liv stayed standing, her feet hips' width apart and her hands clasped behind her back. This seemed acceptable to Haro since he gave her a minute nod, striding over to a table set up with beverages.

"I'm very impressed that you and Warrior Ludwig slew the master demon," Haro said, pouring clear liquid from a decanter into small sake glasses.

"Thank you," Liv stated. "I won't say that was easy, but now that it's done, hopefully, Stefan's job will be more manageable."

Haro handed her a drink. "A Warrior's job will never be easy. When we blot out one evil, something rises up to replace it."

"That's a cynical view." Liv lifted the sake to her nose, the fragrance constricting her nostrils at once. She wasn't a fan of sake, but she also didn't want to be rude. After taking a tiny sip, she kept her reaction to the strong liquor off her face.

Haro held up his glass, nodding to her as if they were toasting. "That it is. However, we exist as the House of Seven to keep balance among the world."

Liv took another sip, wondering where this was going. She trusted Akio, but Haro was different. He'd voted for her to go to the kingdom of the Fae and hunt demons, two cases that many of the Councilors thought would take her out.

"You have created quite a stir among the council members," Haro observed.

"Is that why you asked me here?" Liv asked.

Haro shook his head. "We will get to that in a moment. I simply wanted to point out the obvious. Adler thinks you have a disregard for authority."

Liv laughed, unable to stop herself. "I have a distaste for dumb laws and imposing our will on other magical creatures."

"You speak about justice the same way your mother did," Haro stated, finishing his drink. "She often said that the council pushed laws but ignored justice."

"What do you think?" Liv asked.

"I think it isn't black and white," Haro explained. "Some laws may be outdated. Do we overstep our bounds? It is hard to know, since our perspective is the only one that we see clearly. The council does its best to understand where our Warriors' efforts might best be used, but we are invariably biased."

"Don't you think that too often we ignore the laws that

aren't convenient for us, but reinforce the ones that benefit magicians?" Liv asked.

"What I'm more curious about is that you do," Haro said, sitting crossed-legged on the cushion on the ground.

"Why would that be of interest to you?" Liv asked. It was uncomfortable looking down at Haro, so whether he had intended to force the issue or not, she took a seat across from him so that they were eye-level.

"Warrior Beaufont, it has been a long time since we've had a fresh perspective in the House," Haro began. "Yes, we've had new families join us. The Ludwigs are relatively new. However, they were raised immersed in the world of magic."

"I was too," she argued.

His lips quirked in a contrary smile. "You were, but no one would call your parents or the home they kept typical among magicians. Your parents, much like you, did things their own way and therefore I believe their children think independently of the House doctrine."

Liv wanted to argue that Clark only thought for himself when he was told to, but refrained from making the jab at her brother.

"I had the pleasure of working with Ian and Reese, and I apologize for their deaths," Haro said matter-of-factly. "However, I believe that your time away from the House has created certain advantages for you. I understand you left because you didn't like how the council conducted business."

"They closed the investigation on my parents' death prematurely," Liv argued, cutting him off. Haro hadn't been on the council at that time, but his father was. If he took offense to this slight on his father's decision-making, it didn't show on his face.

"And this is what I mean," Haro said proudly. "I suspect that no one has challenged the council in this way in quite some time. That's a unique quality to you that I've come to appreciate."

"So you don't find it disruptive in our meetings?" Liv asked, surprised to hear Haro say that.

He shook his head. "That's my agenda behind having this discussion with you. I think the worst thing you could do at this point is to conform to the standards of the council."

"Are you encouraging me to rebel and make fun of Adler at meetings?" Liv dared to ask.

With an amused glint in his eyes, Haro said, "I'd never say such a thing. However, I've noticed that your rejecting the status quo and challenging orders is creating a shift. This ripple might be overdue. And I think that your time away from the House of Seven has given you a certain objectivity that is needed at this stage in our history."

"I don't understand," Liv said, scratching her head. "I thought the council was all about order, but you're secretly telling me to remain a rebel. Is that right?"

"Did you know that my grandmother was an Oracle?" Haro asked.

Liv shook her head.

"Yes, in her time, many thought that she was just a crazy, old woman who spoke nonsense," Haro explained. "It wasn't until many of her prophecies came to pass that she was respected for her visions."

"It's amazing how many people who are thought crazy

are actually intelligent, seeing that which the rest of us don't," Liv offered.

"Well put, Warrior Beaufont," Haro stated. "Grandmother Kazuko made many, many prophecies about the future, but they were lost."

"Lost?" Liv asked, leaning forward suddenly. "How is that possible?"

"We didn't have as much magical tech at the time," Haro imparted. "It was my father's generation that imposed that on the House of Seven."

"You say that like you don't agree with its use," Liv observed.

"Much like your parents, I saw the limitations to binding our magic with technology," Haro stated. "We know how unharnessed magic responds to electronics. I'm not sure where I stand on it presently. Sometimes simply knowing that you don't know is enough."

Haro spoke in riddles much like his brother, Liv observed.

"There's a quote that says, 'There are years that ask questions and years that answer,'" she related, remembering the line from *Their Eyes Were Watching God*.

Haro nodded. "And there is a Japanese proverb that says, 'A frog in a well does not know the great sea.'"

The look of confusion on Liv's face triggered Haro to keep talking. "I mean that the House has been limited for a long time. We make judgments based on our experiences, and I believe them to be too narrow. For instance, most of us don't socialize with mortals, as you do. We do not keep the company of other magical races. We are frogs in a well."

"And that's why you're encouraging me to continue to be myself?" Liv asked, and then laughed. "I'm not sure I could stop even if I tried. Being a thorn in Adler's foot gives my life meaning."

"I suspect you are correct, but I also know that some on the council crave the order you disrupt continuously."

And they were finally to it, Liv thought. This was what this meeting was about. The council was talking more openly about how to "manage" Liv.

"As I was saying before," Haro began, "Grandmother Kazuko made many predictions. I'm not sure what happened to those records, but thankfully, in the Takahashi family, we have a tradition of storytelling to preserve our history. It was my ancestors' intention that if something destroyed our history, it could still be preserved in our memories. For that reason, my mother passed along many of the stories her mother told her."

"And those were prophecies?" Liv asked, wondering what had happened to the records. Once again, something of major importance had disappeared. She'd make a killing if she opened a Lost-and-Found office for magicians.

"Yes, and one such prophecy spoke about a Warrior for the House of Seven," Haro imparted. "Grandmother Kazuko foresaw that this person would create much friction among its members, but in doing so, would unearth something that would shatter the very foundation we stand on."

"That person sounds like they will ruin everything," Liv related with a morbid laugh.

"For those who enslave, the revolutionary *does* ruin everything," Haro said, his tone quite serious. "The rebel who overthrows the dictator also rocks the foundation, and yet, without them, justice often goes unserved."

"Who do you think your grandmother was referring to?" Liv asked.

Haro lowered his chin with a look that said, "Who do you think?" on his face.

"I get that I'm disruptive and do things my own way, like the Frank Sinatra song, but I'm not sure I'm the person in this vision of the future," Liv stated.

Haro shrugged like he half-agreed with her. "It's impossible to know." He licked his lips, his eyes skating to the side. "I'm sure it's not you, since the prophecy said this Warrior would hold a giant-forged sword." His eyes darted to Bellator on her hip. "That wouldn't be you, would it?"

Liv tensed. Gulped. Shook her head. "No, that's not me. But it is an interesting prophecy."

"Yes, it is," Haro agreed. "And I think we're overdue for a revolution. Many, I suspect, believe that, but to say it outright seems foolish."

"I sense that the Councilors don't like to oppose Adler and the power he seemingly wields."

Haro nodded. "Adler does have a certain control over the council. It is somewhat of a mystery to me, yet I've unknowingly bowed to it often, although I'm not entirely sure why."

"It sounds like Adler has the council brainwashed," Liv stated.

He had an uncertain expression on his face. "I'm not sure."

"Is that why you voted for me to go on death missions,

like to the kingdom of the Fae and demon hunting, when I wasn't fully trained yet?" Liv asked.

Haro smiled for the first time ever, looking much like his brother. "Oh, no. I voted for you to go on those missions of my own accord."

"Because you want me dead?" Liv joked.

He shook his head. "No. I voted for you to get stronger, and I believe you have."

CHAPTER TWENTY-ONE

"That prophecy is about you, isn't it?" Sophia asked Liv as they strode down the sidewalk to Rory's house.

Clark's paranoia had started to get to Liv, making her look over her shoulder every so often, worried for Sophia. She'd okayed the trip with him prior to them leaving the House of Seven, as they'd agreed. When he told her to "be careful" for the fifth time, she nearly clocked him. However, now that she was out in the middle of the day with the most impressive young magician in the world, fear was setting in. If someone knew what Sophia could do, they'd... Liv couldn't allow herself to think like that. Nothing was ever going to happen to Sophia. Liv would never allow it.

"I'm not so sure," Liv said, wondering if she should have told Sophia so many details. However, she and Clark had agreed to be completely honest with each other, and she felt that included Sophia. If she hadn't been so advanced for her age, Liv could rationalize keeping the truth from her, but Sophia deserved more. She'd earned it. And more than anything, Liv really did value the little magician's opinion.

Sophia pointed to the sword on her hip, which was glamoured so mortals couldn't see it as they passed them on the street. "Isn't Bellator giant-made?"

"Yeah, but we have no clue how many Warriors have had a giant-forged sword."

Sophia pursed her lips, giving Liv a skeptical expression. "Okay, but what other Warriors question the council at every turn?"

"Mom did," Liv chirped.

Sophia nodded. "But she didn't have a giant-made sword."

"No, she had one specifically made for her by an elf, apparently," Liv said, remembering seeing a sword on her mother's hip when she strode in at night, her hair windswept and her eyes dazzling with adrenaline from doing whatever it was that she did as a Warrior. Inexorabilis was apparently an incredible sword that possessed many powers. The thought brought many memories rushing back to the surface: Liv watching her mother sharpen Inexorabilis in front of the fire, Guinevere regarding the sword with pride as it hung on the wall, the weapon sending a shock of electricity to Liv when she accidentally brushed against it while hugging her mother.

"She died with that sword, didn't she?" Sophia asked.

Liv thought for a moment. "Supposedly. I wouldn't think she'd have left it behind."

Thinking about her mother and her sword, made

everything Akio had been trying to convey to her about a Warrior's weapon sink in.

"I bet you're the Warrior who is supposed to rock the foundation of the House of Seven," Sophia said as they rounded the corner to Rory's house.

"I believe Haro said this person would shatter the foundation, not just rock it," Liv corrected.

"Wow, you're going to be a legendary Warrior," Sophia said with a gasp. "Like, they'll write tons of history books about you."

Liv shook her head. "No, there *is* no history of Warriors, or really anyone in the House of Seven, remember? I've been searching, and it all has disappeared, or was never written, or fell into the same hole as the prophecies Haro's grandmother foretold."

"Well, but then you come along and change everything, and after that, there is a history," Sophia said, her blue eyes twinkling with excitement.

"Actually, I'm not sure why Haro would tell me this," Liv said, finally having had a chance to mull over her conversation with the magician. "Someone who shatters the foundation of the House of Seven sounds like an enemy. That person sounds lethal."

"Then why would Haro tell you about it and also encourage you to continue to do things your way?" Sophia questioned.

"I don't know," Liv said, shaking her head as they climbed the porch to Rory's front door. "I'm not entirely sure he can be trusted."

The door to Rory's house peeled back as they

approached, just like it always did. For that reason, Liv usually reasoned that the giant knew they were there and that was his way of welcoming them. However, that didn't explain why he was wearing tights and doing yoga in the middle of his living room.

As Liv often found herself doing when visiting, she halted and looked at the giant in disbelief. "Ummm, what are you doing?"

Sophia giggled, covering her mouth as Junebug darted out from behind the sofa and sprinted under Rory, who was in downward facing dog.

"I'm trying to remember if there are any instructions I need to relay to you before you set off," he said, his voice gruff from being upside down.

Liv glanced down at Sophia, enjoying the smile on the little girl's face as Junebug, made an attempt to play with Rory's dangling curls.

"Ummm...no, I think we're wondering why you're doing yoga in the middle of your living room," Liv stated.

"I'm stretching my calves," Rory said, widening out his stand and pedaling out his feet.

"He's always doing something unexpected," Liv told Sophia.

The young magician dropped the bag she was carrying and joined Rory, stretching into downward facing dog. "I think this is a great idea. Liv, you should join us."

"I would, but I left my yoga pants at the store, along with Rory's giant card," Liv stated, crossing her arms over her chest.

Rory walked his hands up and stood, his face red. "Yoga

is an ancient practice that connects the breath to the body, creating space."

Sophia popped up beside him, her blonde curls falling into her face. "And I don't think that Rory doing yoga makes him any less of a giant."

"It does," Rory stated before Liv could. "Giants are very closed-minded about these kinds of things. My mum raised me very differently than most, offering me an education that was quite unique."

Liv elbowed Sophia in the side. "He went to finishing school."

Rory rolled his eyes at her. "Mum just didn't think I needed to act like a barbarian. She was tired of the stereotypes, and wanted to give me different opportunities."

"And in doing so, she created a giant who doesn't fit in with his own kind," Liv observed.

"I don't want to fit in," he argued.

"Ditto," Liv said with a wink.

"So we should be grateful for parents who gave us more holistic educations," Sophia added.

Rory gave her a look of disbelief.

Liv laughed. "I know. I'm pretty sure she's an imposter, pretending to be an eight-year-old. She sure doesn't speak like one."

"Speaking of imposters," Rory began, "were you able to complete the spell to disguise Liv?"

Sophia nodded, retrieving her bag. "Yes, but first I have a question. Have any other Warriors had a giant-made sword?"

Rory combed his hand through his hair. "I don't know

how that would be possible. Giants don't interact with magicians—"

"Except for you," Liv cut in.

"Well, and as we discussed, I'm different," Rory said.

"And he used to really dislike me," Liv told Sophia with a wink.

"What do you mean, 'used to?'" Rory asked, mock-seriously.

"You totally love me, and you know it," Liv stated.

"I tolerate you better than I used to," he amended before glancing at Sophia. "And to further answer your question, giant-forged swords aren't just floating around for any magician to get hold of. They are guarded, and there aren't many out there since the art form is dying out. With no recent wars, there hasn't been any need to craft swords. My grandfather was the last famous swordsmith."

"But he taught you how to make swords and imbue giant magic into them," Liv stated.

"Yes, but no one knows that," Rory said. "Not even Mum."

"Then there you go," Sophia said, starting to pull objects out of her bag. "The prophecy *is* about you."

"Prophecy?" Rory asked, looking at Liv with worry.

She explained what Haro had told her. The worry on his face deepened as she told him the story.

"Another missing piece of history," he said almost to himself. "This can't be good."

"But don't you think this oracle was referring to Liv?" Sophia asked.

"Oh, most definitely," Rory said with a visible shiver. "I

only worry about the aftermath to the magical population after she's done shattering the House of Seven."

Liv sighed loudly. "Come on, guys. This is ridiculous. I'm not shattering anything except for fashion rules."

"You defeated Sabatore," Sophia argued.

Liv shook her head. "That was Stefan."

"And she found the hidden room with the magical canisters," Rory said to Sophia, nodding.

"Not to mention that bit you guys learned about the missing history of the war between mortals and magicians," Sophia added.

Liv wanted to scream or stomp her feet, or maybe both. "Seriously, you all have listening problems. I'm a dumb Warrior who is simply a placeholder until Sophia the Great takes over for me."

"That's in twelve years," Sophia argued.

"Eleven years and four months, actually," Liv corrected.

Rory drummed his fingers on his lips, thinking. "I suspected this might be coming, but with everything that's happened, I fear the revolution will start before we're prepared."

"What do you have to do?" Liv asked. "Make pies?"

Rory huffed. "Whatever disrupts the House of Seven will have far-reaching effects on the other magical creatures. We'll have to be prepared for that."

"Well, I'm the one holding the sledgehammer, according to you two," Liv said with a laugh. "So what am I supposed to do?"

"Let us know before you swing it," Rory stated with a rare smile.

"Are you ready to become a grumpy old man?" Sophia said, holding up a potion bottle and eyeing the contents.

"When you put it that way, no, absolutely not," Liv said.

A map appeared in Rory's hand. "You'll need this to find the giants."

"I thought they were located on the Isle of Man," Liv said, taking the map. "I thought that was a well-documented area."

"It is, but the area where the giants are is protected by the same magic as my house," Rory explained.

"So someone has to have the exact location, written down specifically for their eyes for you to find," Liv guessed.

"Yes, which is why Decar would make the most sense for going on this mission," Rory stated.

"Then how does the council expect me to find the place?" Liv asked.

Rory gave her an annoyed expression. "I think at this point, they suspect you'll figure it out."

"And they probably know you have a giant friend," Sophia said. "You two are always together."

Liv pursed her lips. "He doesn't think of me as a friend, and they wouldn't see us together because Rory always glamours himself when we're in public together. Maybe it's because his hair is atrocious."

"It's because I'm embarrassed to be seen with you," Rory countered.

"Because I'm dressed like a homeless person?"

"Exactly," Rory stated.

"Okay, so I have the map that will get me on the island

and to where the crazed giants are roasting tourists over a fire," Liv said. "Then what?"

"Then you have to treat them like Decar would," Rory stated.

"Like I'm awesome and they are second-class citizens," Liv supplied.

"Exactly," Rory affirmed. "Decar would only ever talk to the chief, who is the meanest giant I've ever met."

"I'm supposed to tell this guy off?" Liv questioned.

"Yes, exerting your superiority over him as his legion of giants watch," Rory said.

"Why exactly did I sign on for this?" Liv asked.

"Because you're dumb?" Rory offered.

"Because you wanted to protect Turbinger," Sophia countered.

"Well, you told your mother that I'm coming, right?" Liv asked Rory. "Bermuda will help me if things go wrong, won't she?"

"Mrs. Laurens," he corrected. "And no. I figured it would be better if she didn't know. She's not that enamored of you, and would probably urge them to flay you if the opportunity presented itself."

Liv made a great show of bowing to the giant. "I'm ever so grateful to be risking my life for your people."

"Don't mention it," he said dismissively, giving his attention to Sophia. "The disguise: how long will it last?"

"Depending on Liv's stress level, anywhere from one to three hours," Sophia answered.

"Wait, what?" Liv asked.

"The spell is dependent on your mood," Sophia

explained. "The more stressed you are, the less effective it is. So you have to remain calm, or it won't last long."

Liv closed her eyes and clenched her fists. "Okay, do it to me. I'm ready to become a grumpy old albino."

"I need you to drink this potion first," Sophia explained, shoving a vial into Liv's hand.

"What is this?" she asked, opening her eyes again.

"It's a blanking potion."

"That's very smart, Sophia," Rory complimented the girl.

"Thank you," she said with a smile. "I thought the disguising spell would have a better chance of working if we first blanked Liv's appearance."

"What are you two loons talking about?" Liv asked, eyeing the purple sludge in the vial.

"The potion erases…well, *you*, which will make it easier for me to imprint Decar's appearance onto yours," Sophia said.

"Oh, erasing me," Liv said, downing the potion. "So no big deal then."

"Well, there's a chance that what makes you *you* could be gone forever," Sophia warned.

Liv nearly choked on the awful-tasting substance.

"But I'm sure that won't happen," Sophia assured Liv in a rush. "It's just an extra precaution."

Liv expected to disappear as she had when Sophia had made her invisible. Instead, she turned opaque, like she'd stepped into a cloud. "Okay, this is weird."

"It's about to get weirder," Sophia warned, pointing her finger at her sister as she squeezed her eyes shut. "Here goes nothing."

"You mean, 'everything,'" Liv corrected, feeling her form change. Her eyes rose up in the air, and she felt completely different all over, exactly as if she'd stepped into a new body.

Liv looked down at the black robes and long fingers on her hands, flexing them. "Oh, gross. I'm an uptight jerk who doesn't shower often enough."

Sophia smiled broadly at her sister. "Yep, you look perfect. Just like Decar."

CHAPTER TWENTY-TWO

Liv stepped through the portal, nearly losing her footing on the loose rocks in the cave on the shore of the Isle of Man. She wasn't used to being so tall or lanky and didn't like being so far from the ground.

"You need to walk with a certain confidence," Plato offered, eyeing her with amusement from his perch atop a large rock.

"When I'm traversing mossy rock?" she questioned.

"Always," Plato offered. "Right now, you're walking like this isn't your body and you're not used to it."

"I'm not," Liv agreed.

"But Decar is, and the giants will notice if he doesn't seem at ease."

Liv knew he was right. "I just don't know what to do with all these arms and legs. This guy takes up entirely too much room."

"And he's not that nice to look at," Plato said, turning his attention to the ocean beating against the nearby shore.

"You're so superficial," Liv remarked. "So you wouldn't be Decar's friend because he's homely?"

"And he's an uptight magician," Plato added.

"And why again did you randomly befriend me all those years ago after I left the House of Seven?"

"I'd love to answer that question, but I've got to be going." Plato disappeared.

Liv shook her head and Decar's long white hair swayed against her back. "You're never going to answer that question," Liv said, knowing that Plato was probably still there, just invisible. Anyway, that's what she suspected, although she had little idea how his magic worked. She wasn't holding out hope that he'd one day tell her, or even divulge why he had attached himself to her. Maybe it was because she didn't want to push him away with too many serious questions. Or what if the reason was something that spoiled it for her? What if he was her friend because she was a Royal of the House of Seven? What if it had nothing to do with who she was independent of her heritage?

When she started out of the cave, Liv saw what had made Plato leave suddenly, besides avoidance of her questions. There was a tortoiseshell cat strolling down the beach. Unlike Plato, this feline didn't have a tail, and the cat's back legs were longer than her front, making her resemble a rabbit. Liv had heard of this breed of cat, which was called "Manx." They had evolved on the Isle of Man, developing a genetic modification as many breeds do when they are confined to a specific place. They'd lost the tail, not needing it, and gained superior jumping skills.

"Why in the world Plato dislikes cats, I'll never know," Liv said aloud, smiling at the cat, who looked up as she strode by. Rory had said it was because they were in their pure form and that intimidated Plato, but there had to be more to it.

Pulling out the map Rory had given her, she made her way toward the green hills inland. Climbing through the rocks and sand wasn't an easy feat since Decar didn't enjoy the excellent physical health she did. Sophia had stated that although she was still in her body, the disguising spell made it so she shared some of his physical makeup. That was why she was impacted by his health and smelled the weird sour milk scent that wafted off his hair and skin. The dude could also use a good exfoliation. Maybe she'd get him a basket of bath supplies for Christmas.

She laughed to herself, thinking how weird it would be to exchange presents with Decar. He'd probably get her something disgusting like a pair of used socks.

Decar's laugh sounded fake, like it was a sound he wasn't used to making. She climbed through the tall grass on the hillside, enjoying the salt-laced wind. On arrival, Liv had felt the magic on this island. Rory had mentioned that he could feel magic when it was around him. That was how he'd known that her magic had been unlocked. Apparently, giants were more attuned to these things, but all magical creatures could sense it if they tried.

For this reason, the giants would know that Decar was on the island. There was no escaping that. Well, unless she possessed a certain type of stone that hid the presence of magic, but Rory had said they were rare and not worth the effort of having to deal with the elves to get, who he said were too loud and flamboyant.

The map showed that Liv was on the right path,

although she didn't see anything up ahead—only seemingly endless rolling hills. When she came to the top of a steep hill, Liv expected to see the village belonging to the giants at its base, but it just slid down into what appeared to be a rock quarry. The main village full of mortals was to the north. Apparently, they had no idea they shared their island with the majestic giants.

Early on, the House of Seven had tried to require that giants register their magic. Some elfin tribes had willingly done that, and even gnomes weren't that opposed to the requirement in exchange for certain benefits given by the House. Neither magical race was required to do it, as magicians were, but many did, having been pressured or persuaded by the House. However, the giants had declined, confining themselves to the Isle of Man and stating that there they'd go unnoticed by any, so they didn't need to form any alliances with anyone else. According to Rory, the wars that had raged before this separation halted, even though the divide between magicians and giants was still palpable.

Yes, it was good that they weren't fighting, trying to share resources, or conforming to the House's rules. The elves agreed to glamour themselves when they were around mortals. Many magical creatures confined themselves to bubbles within the population, where they went unnoticed by mortals. And on the rare occasion a gnome or fae was seen by a mortal, they usually explained away the incident in some reasonable fashion. Or they ended up being considered "that crazy lady with too many cats."

Liv nearly slid down the slippery hill on the descent. She was glad she didn't, because when she got to the bottom, a rolling village unlike anything she'd ever seen materialized in a wide valley, replacing the rock quarry.

A pristine lake sat at the base of the valley, and around it were colorful fields full of crops, bordered by fruit trees. On the foothills were humble cottages, smoke spiraling up from most of the chimneys.

The village of the giants was simply beautiful. It was modest and inviting and filled Liv with wholesome feelings she hadn't expected. The smell of fresh baked goods and clean water greeted her nostrils. She suddenly couldn't understand why Rory would want to leave this place. It was one of those locations that appeared as though only good things happened there, like an idyllic town where the locals all know each other, protecting one another, spreading goodwill through kind gestures.

An arrow whizzed past Liv's head, making Decar's long white hair fly back in its wake.

She nearly threw herself to the ground to escape what she expected to be a barrage of arrows to follow, but instead, she forced herself to think the strangest thing: *What would Decar do?*

It wasn't a motto that she wanted to live by, but in this instance, it should keep her alive.

Or that was the hope, anyway.

Liv reached into the robes she wore and withdrew the small staff that was apparently Decar's. It grew on both ends until it was full-sized, crowned by a small dragon perched on the top of an opal.

It wouldn't have been safe to bring Bellator into the village, but thankfully Sophia had found a spell that disguised Liv in not only Decar's clothes but also offered her his weapon of choice. Using it would rely solely on her, though, since technically she wasn't holding the staff. It was all an illusion, one that she hoped none of the giants could see through.

Sending out a blast of protective energy, Liv slammed the butt of the staff into the ground, sending a shockwave out around her. The force shot out, knocking several arrows that were flying toward her to the ground. She continued to march forward, careful to keep her chin high and walk with ease even as the ground rumbled under her feet from her spell.

On the front edge of the village, several giants appeared seemingly out of nowhere, holding bows and arrows. They were all male, and wore thick leather clothes. Their hair was French-braided down their backs, and their faces bore unwelcoming expressions.

What Liv did next was against every fiber of her being, but she knew it necessary. She brought the staff up and sent out another blast, this one an offensive measure.

As if a tidal wave had hit the men, who were all over seven feet tall, they fell to the ground. Before they had a chance to get up, Liv strode forward, crossing the space between them faster than she would have thought possible, thanks to Decar's long legs. At least there was finally something good about the old grump's body.

The effect of using such a huge amount of magic was immediately evident. Liv swayed, thinking she might fall over right then. She propped her weight on the staff, covering her exhaustion with a deep scowl.

"I didn't come to fight you, giants," Liv said, her voice

deep and foreboding. "But if you continue to oppose my visit, I'll have no choice but to slaughter you."

The closest giant rolled over, growling as he pushed himself to his feet. Even for someone as tall as Decar, the giant towered over her. However, she had gotten used to that since hanging out with Rory. Well, and also because she'd been vertically challenged all her life.

She lifted her chin, flashing a menace that she'd seen Adler display many, many times.

"You aren't to enter our lands, magician," the giant said, his bright blue eyes narrowing. Most of the giants had blond hair and light-colored eyes. In comparison, Rory would have stuck out among them with his curly dark-brown hair and emerald-green eyes.

"That is Warrior Sinclair to you," Liv said, having a hard time getting out the rude words. However, she was sure that was how Decar would have responded. He'd want the respect he thought he'd deserved. Nothing for him was about building goodwill, but rather intimidation.

"It doesn't matter who you are. You're not welcome here," another giant said, coming to stand next to the first. The others were brushing themselves off or nocking arrows and aiming them at Liv.

"According to the charter we set up long ago," Liv stated calmly, "a Warrior from the House of Seven is allowed entry into this peasant village of yours to offer you an opportunity for a civilized accord."

"But what if no one knows that you entered our village?" the giant in front of her asked, threat in his tone.

Liv stepped up as if she were at eye-level with the huge man, snarling as she'd seen Decar do many times. "Do not forget what I've done to many of your brothers." With a flick of her chin, she sent out another blast, sending the giants behind him back down to the ground like dominos that had been kicked over.

The giant spun, crouching as he checked on his brethren.

Still calm, Liv said, "They aren't dead, but the next time they will be, and you'll join them."

The giant spun back around, his cheeks flushed with anger.

Even though Liv didn't presently have the strength to do that again, at least not for a few moments, she held up Decar's staff intimidatingly.

The giant seemed to consider Decar, maybe deciding whether to believe the threat.

"Take me to your chief," Liv ordered. "I don't have all day to waste away in this place."

For a moment, Liv worried that she'd gone too far. Insulting the giants pained her, but she knew that was exactly how Decar would treat them. And Rory had been right—they *would* have roasted her from the beginning. However, Decar's intimidation won out. The giant held up a huge hand, directing Decar to the large gate in front of the village.

"Go on then, Warrior Sinclair," the giant said. "I will lead you to Chief Dag."

Liv couldn't believe it had worked. If allowed, she would have entered the village as herself, with respect and consideration for who the giants were. She would have offered to protect them, forging a path to a better life among the magical creatures. She would have explained the life that she and Rory had talked about, full of respect for others.

However, this was still a world run by men with giant egos. And for now, it was better that they believed her to be one of them: Decar Sinclair.

CHAPTER TWENTY-THREE

The gate rolled back, pulled by thick ropes. As it opened, Liv found many giants staring at her from the other side. They created a long procession, none of them wearing welcoming faces.

She strode behind the giant who had acted like the leader, her chin high and a snooty expression on her face. Twice she nearly tripped on Decar's long robes, the exhaustion from her magical efforts making each movement difficult.

Reaching into the pocket of her robes, Liv found the Reese's Pieces that Sophia had snuck in there for her. She grabbed a handful and nonchalantly slipped them into her mouth.

Chewing with Decar's mouth was probably the worst part of being him. His teeth didn't fit together right, and he had a loose crown in the back. *Dude should really take better care of his teeth,* she thought, nearly laughing at the image of Decar wearing clunky braces. She wondered if the giants would be as intimidated by him if he spoke with a lisp and wore headgear. Sadly, she suspected that they'd still take him more seriously looking like that than they would her.

If they only knew that the magician who had flattened them twice was a young woman. Liv shook off her frustration and reminded herself of why she was there, risking her life for this mission. It was to ultimately protect the giants, who had reasons for reacting the way they did to magicians.

The crowd parted as the giant in front of Liv charged forward. Although Liv was eager to study the thatch-roofed houses, creative buildings that blended into the hillsides, and the giants gawking at her, she kept her focus forward. Showing curiosity or appreciation for their village was not something Decar would do. He wouldn't be the least bit curious about how the giants modestly lived.

She caught sight of a few women. They were dressed similarly to the men, in thick animal pelts and leather pieces sewn together with rope. Like the men, they wore their light-colored hair in braids, making it somewhat difficult to tell the difference between the genders. The only thing that made it slightly easier was that the men were a bit taller than the women.

When they had reached the middle of the village, they came to an arch covered in lush flowers. Liv hadn't expected to enter a garden, or find it absolutely breathtaking if she had. Now more than ever, it was hard not to look around as they entered an area that was sectioned off from the rest of the village by stone walls.

Rory's garden was impressive, overflowing with many varieties of vegetables and foliage, but it paled in comparison to this one. The scents of sweet nectar and rich soil wafted through the air, reminding Liv of running through the garden at the House of Seven when she was a child, sprinting away or after Clark.

The giant in front of Liv stopped abruptly, nearly causing her to run into him. That was mostly because she'd allowed her eyes to wander over the many interesting plants growing robustly from the earth. Most of them she'd never seen before. Everywhere were strange plants with intricate patterns on their leaves or large bulbs of various neon colors, looking ready to burst. Not only that, but birds with yellow beaks and blue underbellies flew around the flowers, making sounds like children chatting. Liv wouldn't have believed that this place was real if she wasn't seeing it with her own eyes. Well, Decar's.

Another giant stepped onto the cobbled path, and Liv found herself standing in front of the largest one she'd yet to meet. Chief Dag was dressed in a cape that reached the ground. It would have taken many animal skins to make; a single buffalo would not have that much hide. Unlike most in the village, this giant had reddish-brown hair and bushy eyebrows which were scrunched together as he regarded the magician before him.

Behind the chief were more arbors that led to different paths. The garden seemed to go on and on, each trail leading to a different adventure that Liv longed to explore. She shook off her curiosity, arranging her face into an expression of pure disdain. It instantly made her feel bitter. No wonder her parents had told her never to scowl. Putting on the expression brought on the emotions associated with it.

Behind the chief crouched a giant who was digging in

the dirt. Unlike everyone else she'd encountered on the island, this giant was wearing a floral print shirt and a bonnet on her head. Liv couldn't make out the giant's face, but she guessed it was a woman based on the soft curls spilling around the collar of her shirt.

Chief Dag opened his mouth to speak, but Liv cut him off at once with a tired sigh—the same one Adler often released in her presence. "It has come to the House of Seven's attention that the one-hundred-year mark is upon us again," she said, withdrawing the treaty the council had given her from her robes. "As we so thoughtfully promised, we're giving the giants a chance to join the elves and gnomes in an alliance with the magicians."

Chief Dag narrowed his eyes. "From what I understand, the elves are presently questioning their alliance with you."

Liv hadn't expected this. Was this what the council had been busy with when she and Stefan had delivered the report from demon hunting? She recovered quickly, "How would you know what the elves are doing?"

The crouched figure stood and spun around. "I told him," Bermuda Laurens said.

Liv didn't know why she hadn't recognized Rory's mother. The last time she'd seen Bermuda, she'd been wearing a similar getup and a large hat. Liv had thought that Bermuda was only wearing regular clothes because she was visiting Los Angeles. She hadn't expected her to be dressed like a cheery grandmother among her own people.

Hiding her surprise, Liv said, "And how would you know?"

Sticking her meaty hands on her hips—and smearing

dirt on her floral print shirt—Bermuda pursed her lips. "I know better than most, Decar Sinclair."

"Our negotiations with the elves are none of your business, Bermuda," Liv replied, putting an inflection on the giant's name.

Bermuda regarded Decar for a long moment, and something flickered behind her eyes. "Old age is treating you well, magician. Why your magic has increased since the last time you cursed us with your presence?"

Liv tensed at the question. Bermuda could feel her magic? Would she figure out that Decar wasn't here? Damn Rory's mother for being so smart and observant.

"Unlike you giants," Liv said, thinking fast, "living in a proper place provides us with numerous benefits. But I wouldn't expect you to understand that."

Bermuda laughed and wiped the back of her hand over her forehead. "I see that your old age has done nothing to increase your diplomacy or tact."

"Nor has it made you any more attractive," Liv quipped.

Bermuda pursed her lips, turning her attention to Chief Dag.

"I think I've fixed your infestation problem with the snorbs," she said. "The gideons should make a full recovery."

Chief Dag nodded. "Thank you, Bermuda."

She picked up her gardening tools before offering Liv one more look of disdain.

When she'd stomped off, Liv shook the treaty at the chief. "Do you want to be included in the alliance or not? I don't have all day."

Actually, Liv was more concerned about shifting back

into her normal form. It had been over an hour since Sophia had done the spell on her, and it was unclear how long it would last. Liv had been told that stress was a factor, and she couldn't deny that her level of tension was higher than usual. How could it not be, when she was surrounded by brooding giants who would like nothing better than to stomp out an evil magician?

"Under the present circumstances, the giants have no interest in working with you magicians," Chief Dag said, twirling his large finger in the air. "I suspect that in the future, you'll *have* no alliances, especially if you keep strong-arming all the others."

Liv unrolled the parchment to find that the Chief had magically given up their option for the next one hundred years, so she was almost done. All she had to do was make her exit.

"I don't know what you mean," Liv said. "We simply offer the others the protection you've declined."

"Were you protecting those elves in the north that you slaughtered for disagreeing with you, Decar Sinclair?" Chief Dag asked, his voice booming.

Liv was knocked off-guard momentarily, not expecting this misdirection. "That's not what happened."

The chief nodded. "What you mean to say is that there isn't any proof, but the rumors are clear about what happened. How can you expect anyone to negotiate with you when you exert your power, striking down anyone who would disagree with you?"

"That's not what happened," Liv repeated.

Decar had killed a bunch of elves? No wonder the council needed an extra advantage working with the elves.

"In one hundred years, don't return to this island," the Chief stated. "We will send our refusal to associate with magicians well in advance." He lifted his hand, pointing at the exit. "Leave the village of the giants now."

Liv knew better than to say a word, even using Decar's voice. A bully could only get away with so much for so long. She feared she might not make it out of the village before the giants decided to pool their strength, striking down the evil magician, who even she thought deserved to be punished. What would have caused him to murder elves? For disagreeing? That couldn't be the whole story. She needed to find out more.

When Liv turned around, the crowd at her back parted. She picked up her pace, pretending she was leaving of her own accord. Decar wouldn't tuck tail and run. Instead, he'd hold his head unnecessarily high and sweep through the village like it was he who couldn't stand to be there one moment longer.

When Liv stepped to the other side of the large gate, they almost shut it on her heels. She hurried over the hills, knowing that the portal couldn't be created until she was close to the water. The giants had certain wards around their village, and water was a powerful conduit for portals that increased their power, making them easier to use. That would be necessary for Liv since she currently lacked much of her strength.

She popped another handful of Reese's Pieces into her mouth, chewing rapidly before swallowing quickly.

When she was over the last ridge and the ocean was only a few yards away, Plato appeared. Relief filled her stomach, making her smile. The expression probably appeared strange on the old man's face, and Liv wondered if that was why Plato was giving her a strange look. A moment later he disappeared without saying a word.

"I get that he's an ugly mudder, but you can handle looking at him a little longer," Liv said, noticing that her hands were now her own. She was starting to turn back. The timing couldn't have been any better.

With her legs changing back to normal, she nearly tumbled down the embankment leading to the beach. It was harder than before to negotiate the path to the cave.

When Liv had finally made it into the shelter of the cave, she realized that the hair on her shoulders was shorter, healthier, and blonde. She was nearly back to normal. Drawing in a breath, she prepared to create a portal home.

"I knew it was you," a voice behind her said, making her freeze.

CHAPTER TWENTY-FOUR

If running had been an option, Liv would have done it, putting as much distance between her and the person at her back as possible. However, she was in a cave, with potentially a lot of dead ends ahead of her. Not only that, but she was pretty sure one of her legs was longer than the other since she was still changing back, making running on the rocky shore difficult and also dangerous. And she wasn't sure she could make a portal with her heart beating as rapidly as it was.

Therefore she reluctantly turned to face Bermuda Laurens. Liv wasn't sure at first that she'd heard the voice correctly, with the ocean winds howling past her ears. However, when she turned, she confirmed what she'd expected.

With her hands on her hips and an unsatisfied expression on her face, Bermuda regarded her with ultimate contempt.

"What exactly are you doing here?" the giant asked. There was still dirt smeared on her chin.

Liv couldn't even imagine how ridiculous she looked right then, halfway between her form and Decar Sinclair's. She smiled meekly, but it probably looked very wrong on her face. "So, funny story—"

"I don't want a story," Bermuda said, cutting her off. "That's what magicians tell others when they want to deceive them. Tell me the truth, Warrior Beaufont."

"The council was going to send Decar Sinclair to discuss the treaty with Chief Dag," Liv began in a rush. "However, I knew that if he came to the Isle of Man, he'd sense Turbinger, creating even more problems for us, especially because you didn't tell anyone that it's been recovered. And in not doing so, conveniently forgot to mention to anyone that I recovered it. That made it pretty impossible for me to go on this goodwill mission, since the giants would have never allowed me entry. And worst of all, Decar would have come here and caused more problems, killing more innocent magical creatures. So Rory came up with the idea that I'd come disguised as Decar, who the giants will strangely deal with. The plan was to get the treaty declined formally by Chief Dag so the giants got to live in peace without interference from magicians for another hundred years. And now the mission is accomplished, and the giants are safe, along with Turbinger."

Bermuda regarded the Warrior for a long few moments, her eyes searching Liv's. "Are you looking for a thank you?"

"Mostly I'm just hoping that you'll quit treating me like I'm an awful reject," Liv dared to say.

"If you're doing all this to win my boy's heart, it won't work."

Liv couldn't stop the laugh that burst from her mouth. "Did you think… Oh, my god, Rory and me? You've got to be kidding."

"He's the best catch the likes of you could hope for," Bermuda stated.

"He's my friend," Liv argued.

"Magicians don't have giants as friends," Bermuda said. "They use them, and discard of them when they are done."

"Although I know you have had many experiences that would make you believe that, it's not true for Rory and me," Liv objected. "He's helping me. Well, we're helping each other. We want to find out what the House of Seven has been covering up and fix things."

"I've held Turbinger, and know that what you seek to fix is impossible," Bermuda said. She took a step forward, making Liv take a step back.

"How can uncovering forgotten history be impossible?" Liv asked. "All we need is evidence. This is just the beginning of the search. There are many places left to look."

Bermuda shook her head of soft brown curls. "Because it's been buried too long. I tried at one point while I was writing my book, and it didn't end well."

"What?" Liv asked in disbelief, noticing that the tide was rising. It would lock them in the cave if they weren't careful, slowing drowning them. "You know about all this?"

Bermuda nodded, scorn flashing in her eyes. "I knew that something wasn't right. I started poking around, and my poor husband Gabe, Rory's father, paid the price."

"How is that?" Liv asked.

"The giants believe his transport stone malfunctioned,"

Bermuda explained as the water rushed over her ankles. "That's what Rory believes too, and I have no evidence to the contrary. However, *I* believe that the House of Seven was behind Gabe's death. I'd been warned when I was doing my research to leave certain things alone. Hints had been dropped, but I didn't listen. When Gabe died, I finally did. Somethings aren't worth uncovering, not at the expense of losing those most valuable to you."

"But don't you see?" Liv argued. "Whatever they are covering up, whatever they don't want us to find, we have to do it, no matter what. Others will come after us and try, and meet the same intimidation."

"No, Warrior Beaufont, because this ends here," Bermuda said. "I hold Turbinger. Without it, no one will know what you know."

"But *I* know!" Liv yelled. "I'm not going to forget, and I'm not giving up. Too many have been killed over this. My parents. My siblings. Your husband. Who knows who else?"

A tragic expression overwhelmed Bermuda's face. "I was once like you, wanting to change the world. It's why I wrote *Mysterious Creatures*." She laughed, but the sound held no joy. "I thought I could save the world, but this is much too big. You're better off moving on. Resign from the House, and go off and live a wasteful magician's life. I'd advise against breeding, but your type rarely listens to me on that one."

"I'm not stepping down from the House," Liv stated adamantly. "It's my birthright. The Beaufonts were one of the first families."

Bermuda sighed heavily. "And that pride will make you

one of the last to survive. Whatever they are hiding isn't worth losing everything over."

Liv stomped, then realized she was back to normal. Seawater splashed her face. "I've already lost everything!"

Bermuda shook her head. "No. That's the thing—there is always more to lose. I believe I was spared from being murdered because, unfortunately for the House of Seven and other magicians, they can't deny that I hold certain knowledge that shouldn't die out just yet. I've been asked to document it, as I did in *Mysterious Creatures*, but I know all too well that I would be signing my death warrant. I will not be writing another book, so hopefully, I'll survive long enough to meet my grandkids one day. However, I've been secretly warned that digging in places where I don't belong will result in more deaths."

Liv gasped, realizing she was referring to Rory. "So you gave up the search to protect him?"

"And you will too," Bermuda said, the water up to her calves now.

Liv shook her head furiously. "I won't give up. Have you told Rory this? Maybe he would help you. Maybe he doesn't want you to give up for him."

"My son sees things better than most, but he wouldn't understand. You wouldn't understand the sacrifices that a mother makes to keep her child alive," Bermuda said.

Liv couldn't argue with that, but she knew that she wanted her little sister to grow up in a world different from this one. She wanted equality for all. She wanted justice served in the House of Seven. She wanted Sophia Beaufont's position as Warrior to mean something, and how could that happen if there was a truth buried so deep that no one knew exactly what they were fighting for anymore?

"Olivia Beaufont, I can't allow you to put my son in danger by dragging him into this."

"My name is Liv. And what if he wants to be involved in this?"

A surge of water rushed past Bermuda's knees. "If you've convinced him to join you, then he isn't thinking straight. Both of you must abandon this."

"No!" Liv yelled, her voice echoing in the cave. "Don't you see? If we give up after they've taken so much, then they've won. You've already lost your husband. I've lost my parents and sister and brother. We're exactly in the position to find out the truth. Otherwise, they will all have died for nothing."

Bermuda's great weight was swayed by the rushing tide that was pouring into the cave.

Liv knew that the giant could turn around and swim back out of the cave, but that option was fading fast. They would soon be stuck, and they both knew it. This was the best possible situation in Liv's opinion because, more than anything, she needed Bermuda Laurens on her side, even if she was almost forced to be there.

Daring to put her back to the giant, Liv opened a portal. When it shone brightly, she turned back to Bermuda. "Come with me. Help us."

Rory's mother considered this for a long moment, so long that the next wave nearly knocked Liv over. They had only seconds to get out of the cave before all options were gone.

Liv didn't turn back as she swam through the portal, landing in a heap on Rory's lawn.

He looked up with relief as she choked on the salt water she'd swallowed. However, his expression transformed into pure amazement when his mother fell through the portal, landing rather ungracefully next to them.

CHAPTER TWENTY-FIVE

Since giants weren't supposed to use portal magic, especially at Bermuda's age, the giant fainted seconds after landing in Rory's yard. Liv gave him a quick explanation, but she knew that he cared little why his mother was there and more about her well-being. Not wanting to be in the way, Liv left with a promise to check on them later. Rory didn't seem to care when she returned. He doted on his mother, fanning her as she awoke in his lawn chair. If Liv hadn't already been planning to get out of there, the ridiculously fierce scowl Bermuda offered her upon waking was a good motivator to hightail it out of there.

"It just doesn't make any sense," Liv said, squinting at the electric can opener in front of her on the workbench.

"Well, have you tried turning it off and back on?" Plato asked, sitting beside her.

She rolled her eyes at him. "That's how you fix a computer, and I'm not referring to the can opener."

"I'm not sure which part doesn't make sense," Plato said

matter-of-factly. "People, no matter what race or species, will do anything to protect the ones they love. Bermuda felt intimidated."

"Yes, but what if whatever they are hiding puts everyone we love in *more* danger?"

"Most people are pretty short-sighted," Plato stated.

"Did you hear what the giants said about the elves and Decar?" Liv asked, pushing the can opener aside. She had thought that fixing something would put her head straight, but it wasn't working.

Plato nodded. "Yes, that was disconcerting. Maybe Clark will know more about it."

Liv glanced up, appreciating the renovation that Clark had helped her implement in the shop. Well, he had done it all, but he had taught her how to do expansion magic in the process, which was nice. She was planning on practicing it on her apartment soon.

The narrow shelves that used to be attached to the side of one wall were now an entry to a capacious storage area. The high shelves stretched down the shop for twenty feet, and they also rose to the ceiling. Thanks to a handy lift system, it was easy to retrieve things from up high.

So far none of the customers had questioned the renovations because of the glamour Clark had applied to them. He'd also thrown a new coat of paint on the walls, magically speaking, and redone the flooring as well. The shop looked brand new, and the renovation had imbued John with an even happier demeanor.

Liv heard him whistling in the back, and it made her smile. She knew he'd worried about her a lot more lately due to the magic, so anything she could do to make his life easier was good.

Plato stretched, then stood up. "Well, I'd stay, but you're about to get company. And I can't stand this person."

Liv's head jerked up. "Is it Adler? Decar? What would they be coming here for?"

Plato shook his head. "No, those magicians are despicable, but this person is the absolute worst."

Liv's brow furrowed. "Is it a demon?" she asked, her hand flying to Bellator, which was sitting out of view on a low shelf.

"No, but he smells almost as bad," Plato said, and disappeared as the door to the shop opened and Rudolf entered.

Liv laughed, smelling the overwhelming cologne wafting off the fae.

Rudolf laughed along with her like he hadn't heard the joke but wanted to be involved.

"What did you do to Plato to make him hate you so much?" Liv asked him as he sauntered forward, flipping the collar of his jacket up.

Rudolf halted, sliding up sideways next to the table with a seductive look. "I explained to him why the lynx population is dying out." He cupped his hand to his mouth and leaned forward, whispering, "You see, they are loners, which makes breeding an issue. And they are notoriously bad at romance. I simply told him that if he'd put a bit more effort into his appearance and worked on his bedroom moves, then when the right lynx came around, he'd be ready to seal the deal. Wham! Bam! And then there would be a baby lynx."

Liv shook her head. "I'm shocked that offended him."

Rudolf agreed. "I know, right? You try to help someone! Oh, well, when the time comes, he'll remember what I said about slow-dancing in the moonlight."

"I'm almost certain that he won't," Liv said dryly.

Rudolf glanced at her sharply, like he was not sure he was seeing her correctly. "Did you do something different with your hair?"

Liv tugged on one of the locks, eyeing it. "Nope."

"Is that a new black t-shirt?" he asked, confused. "It looks less threadbare than your other faded black t-shirts."

Liv glanced down and shrugged. "I pulled it off the floor this morning when I rolled out of bed."

Rudolf closed his eyes for a half-beat. "I fear that you'll never breed either, my sweet Liv. You have no style, and you never brush your hair, and your makeup really doesn't work for you."

"I'm not wearing any makeup."

Rudolf threw up his hands. "And now we're uncovering even more problems. I beseech you to never leave your house without at least three layers of eyeshadow. You can't expect a man to like you for your brains with a personality like yours."

Liv stuck her tongue out at him. "Oh, too bad. Well, it appears I'll have to throw myself into my work. If only I had a job or two or three that demanded all of my time."

Rudolf pointed over his shoulder. "There's a cocktail bar I just passed that's hiring. The waitresses wear short little numbers and halter tops, but you might be able to get a job busing tables."

"Do tell me why you're here before I throw you through the front window," Liv said.

"Sure thing—as soon as you tell me why you were using a disguising spell on your pretty face?" Rudolf asked.

Surprised, Liv leaned forward. "How did you know?"

Rudolf laughed, brushing his thumb over her chin like she had leftover crumbs there from her blueberry muffin. "You still have remnants of the old man you were impersonating on you."

Liv slapped his hand away. "You can see that?" She lifted the toaster next to her, peering into its reflective surface.

"Yes, but most can't see those things," Rudolf said. "Fae have a way of seeing remnants of leftover magic, enabling us to detect past spells."

"Wow, that could come in handy," Liv mused.

"Oh, let me tell you about it," Rudolf said. "The next time we're out, I'll point out all the magicians who have used male enhancement spells."

"Please don't," Liv said, shaking her head as she set the toaster down.

"Of course," Rudolf sang, drawing out the words, "Fae don't use those spells since we are very well endowed, if you know what I mean."

Liv feigned confusion. "I don't. Do you mean with large noses? Yours is awfully large."

Rudolf cupped his hand over his nose. "No, I meant—"

"Why are you here, Big Nose?"

Rudolf pulled his hands off his face and reached into his pocket. He pulled out Liv's mother's ring and set it on the worktable between them. "I found the memory connected to this."

The barstool nearly toppled over when Liv shot up. "Are you serious? What is it?"

"Well, there were a few memories of me at dinner parties where I was wearing yellows and oranges, which totally aren't my color," Rudolf stated. "I think I was better without reliving those."

"Jerkface," Liv growled menacingly.

"Okay, fine," Rudolf said. "Most of the memories I unearthed were inconsequential, but then something strange happened. Something I'm not sure how I forgot, or how anyone could."

"Please tell me," Liv encouraged.

He scratched his head. "Liv, this is weird. And I think what I learned is incomplete."

She rolled her eyes. "I get that you're starved for attention, so you're using this in an attempt to draw out this interaction, but get on with it."

He flashed her a brilliant smile. "If only that were true. But I get your point. You know how most mortals will dismiss magic if they see it directly?"

Liv stood straighter. She remembered that John had stated that his ex-wife Chloe had been required to show him magic repeatedly for him to finally see it. This was common, and it was one reason that telling mortals about magic didn't usually work. However, he thought it had worked because they were in love and uniquely bonded. Otherwise, most mortals witnessing magic repeatedly wouldn't do the trick. They simply didn't see it, for whatever reason.

"Yeah, I know what you're talking about," Liv said, having seen this herself many times.

Rudolf nodded, glad she was following. "Well, in these past memories, I learned something quite shocking. Mortals used to know about magic."

Liv tilted her head to the side. "What do you mean?"

"I saw dozens of parties and events; really, I spent way too much of my youth hanging out at lavish affairs. I'm not sure what I was thinking, except that I was obsessed with—"

"Dorkface, get to the freaking point," Liv said, cutting him off.

He nodded. "Anyway, in all of these memories, magicians or fae or whatever magical creatures entertained the masses with spells. Mortals were there as a part of the festivities."

"And they saw the magic?" Liv asked. "Are you sure?"

"I'm quite sure," Rudolf replied.

"How is this connected to the ring?" Liv asked.

"That I'm not sure about," Rudolf stated. "There was more, but that was pretty much the gist. Mortals used to know about magic. I kept your secret, so I didn't ask around if this was news to anyone else, but I assume it would be. For all of my life, before holding your ring, I couldn't remember mortals being at those parties or witnessing magic."

So there had once been a war between magicians and mortals, and now they knew that mortals knew about magic. But why had this war been erased from history? And why couldn't mortals see magic anymore? What had happened? And more importantly, why?

Liv let out a deep breath, aware that Rudolf was gazing

at her with a wide smile. When she got tired of him giving her that dumbass grin, she snapped, "What?"

"Well, it's just that I've done what you asked. I found the memories connected to the ring."

Liv sighed. "And so now you want me to do something for you, right?"

"Yes."

"You want me to retrieve something from the fountain in the House of Seven, correct?" she asked. That didn't seem like such a big deal, although she'd experienced a really strange incident in that fountain as a child. The details were murky.

Rudolf nodded.

"What is it that I'm retrieving?"

"I can't tell you that," he answered.

Liv crossed her arms over her chest. "Oh, no. This is a trick, like before when you took me into that gnome shop and got me in trouble with the Father of Time."

He shook his head. "No, it's not a trick. It's just that it's not important for you to know what you're retrieving, because there is only one thing down there, besides what guards it."

Liv tensed. "Something is guarding it?"

"Naturally. All important things are heavily guarded."

Liv knew how agreements with the fae worked. Rudolf had fulfilled his end of the bargain, so she had to as well, or she'd owe him for ten years of servitude. She reasoned that it didn't really matter what she was retrieving from the fountain. What Rudolf had learned was incredibly valuable. They were that much closer to uncovering the truth.

She did have a couple of questions though, just to cover

her bases. "You say this is important? Will anyone in the House of Seven miss it if I give it to you?"

He shook his head. "No one will know it's gone, but I've missed it for a very, very long time. What resides at the bottom of that fountain is the most important thing in this world to me."

CHAPTER TWENTY-SIX

This was an area of the library that neither Clark nor Liv had seen before. Chandeliers with a hundred candles each illuminated the bookshelves, which were only waist height. On top of them were small replicas of the different rooms in the House of Seven.

"Why have we never seen this before?" Liv asked, running her finger over the spines of the books, amazed by how large this section was.

"Have you ever looked for the history about the physical House of Seven?" Clark countered.

"Well, I've been trying to find history on the Seven for a while," Liv remarked.

"Yes, but you've been looking for information on the families, which is very different from what you're searching for right now."

Liv nodded, studying the model of the dining room. There were models for all the common rooms, but nothing about the Chamber of Tree or the entry or the Black Void. When Liv had thought about that strange and mysterious place between the residential wing and the Chamber of the Tree, the library had literally offered nothing. She'd pulled out books with blank pages. After the third time, she assumed that the library didn't want to give her information on it, or it didn't have any.

The books that had words had provided some of the spells that created and maintained the House. It was incredible to think of the magic that had gone into creating the House, and also keeping it secret from the rest of the world. There were over three thousand wards on the House that kept it protected, although the specifics on those weren't detailed. Liv reasoned that it was a security measure. Maybe that was why there had been nothing when she searched for the history of the founding families, only the wall with the ancient language.

Liv pulled the Warrior ring from her pocket, eyeing the huge piece of jewelry. "When do you want to make our attempt?"

Clark looked back at her, catching her meaning. "Soon. When you're done with this favor for Rudolf. It wouldn't be good to make a fae wait. They can decide on a whim that you didn't fulfill your end of the bargain fast enough and put you in servitude."

For some reason, Liv didn't think that Rudolf would do that. He wanted her to retrieve what was at the bottom of the fountain. However, she didn't argue with Clark. Opening the Ancient Chamber would have to wait until they had a better chance. A part of her worried that it would trigger an alarm when they opened the chamber. It was crucial that no one knew they were collecting information or find out what they knew already. Liv wouldn't be able to handle losing anyone else.

"Have you ever heard of a mortal knowing about magic?" Liv dared to ask Clark in the open area, only because he'd put a silencing spell around them.

Clark glanced around as if he were afraid that someone could still hear them, then shook his head. "It doesn't even seem possible. Do you trust Rudolf?"

Liv hesitated before responding, "He is pretty scummy, but yes. He has no reason to lie about this, and it meshes with the missing history that Rory learned."

Clark let out a weighty breath. "This is getting bigger. With the canisters and what Bermuda told you, I worry that what we learn may not be something we're going to like."

"When we search for the facts, it can't be about finding what we want. It's about discovering the truth. I'm committed to finding that, whether it changes nothing or ruins everything."

"Or shatters the very foundation of the House of Seven," Clark added morbidly, repeating what she'd learned from Haro.

Liv didn't want to think about that. Maybe if the oracle hadn't referred so specifically to her, it wouldn't be so difficult to dismiss.

"I don't understand why the prophecy couldn't have said an uptight Councilor who wears too much hair gel shattered the very foundation of the House of Seven," she remarked as they browsed.

Clark gave her an incredulous glare. "I don't wear too much hair gel."

"You absolutely do," Liv argued. "But enough about you. Tell me about the elves and Decar."

Clark paused, his eyes shifting back and forth with indecision.

"Come on," Liv urged. "I understand that Warriors aren't supposed to know about the things Councilors do, but I've told you all this other stuff."

"This other stuff isn't House business," Clark said in a whisper. "These are secrets that no one is supposed to know, apparently."

"Just tell me about the elves," Liv argued.

"Tell me about you and Stefan," Clark countered.

Liv hitched up her hip, clapping her hand on it. "There's nothing to tell. We hunted demons. Now I'm in between cases."

"The council still doesn't have anything for you," Clark said. "I daresay they don't really know what to do with you at this point. Maybe there is a wild dragon that needs taming, or a comet heading toward Earth that you could stop."

"Ha-ha. I think that half the Councilors didn't expect me to return with all my limbs," Liv joked.

Clark agreed with a nod. "That's because they don't know that you have insider information about the giants. Adler is sure that it was luck, although Bianca checked the treaty you brought back for forgery."

"Oh, I would have liked to have seen her face when she realized it was really Chief Dag's signature," Liv stated.

"I'm serious about Stefan," Clark urged. "There was something off about him before, and now he seems different. Not as bad, but there is still something strange about him."

Liv tucked her chin and pretended to read a book about the various pieces of artwork hanging in the House of Seven.

Clark placed his hand on the book, pushing it down. "Liv, we promised no secrets."

Pulling the book to her chest, Liv shook her head. "It's not my secret to tell, and really of no consequence to you. Otherwise, I'd tell you."

Clark didn't appear satisfied by this answer, but he let it go. "Fine. And I'm not sure what good it would do for you to know about the elves. It was just a one-off altercation. It's unclear what triggered it, but Decar said he was defending himself."

"And in doing so, he killed how many elves?" Liv asked.

"Five."

"And that spoiled the negotiations between the House and the elves?"

Clark massaged his temples like he had a sudden headache. "Things weren't ideal in the first place. You two killing Sabatore did help, but still. More and more of the magical community is starting to distrust the House."

Liv laughed darkly. "That's because we bully everyone. We ignore looting goblins because we have a certain agreement with them. We punish trolls for simply being lost. And we treat our own kind with cruelty for not conforming to laws."

"That's how it works, Liv," Clark stated. "When someone breaks the law, they are punished."

"Has it occurred to you that us registering our magic is wrong?"

"It's a necessary control," Clark argued.

"Why? Because some jerk magician said so?" Liv asked.

"When someone disobeys the law, it's easier to stop them if they are registered," Clark explained.

Liv gave him a cold stare. "Yes, and that works great in a system that isn't corrupt. However, when the House has absolute power, who is keeping *us* in check?"

Clark pointed at her. "You are."

She shook her head and strode away, tired of the same old, same old discussion with her brother. However, there was something that had been bothering her so deeply lately despite all the new revelations that she felt like it was about to burst out of her. She spun around to face her brother.

"There can be no law without sympathy. Justice can't happen without peace in the laws," Liv stated with real conviction in her voice.

She'd gotten Clark's attention now.

"These arbitrary laws don't protect us, which is what they are supposed to do," Liv stated. "They control us, and that's completely different. Our community, and the gnomes and the elves, and especially the giants, aren't at peace. We are simply existing, and sidestepping around each other. Everyone is afraid of us. You'd see that if you set foot in Roya Lane. We're the police force, so no one wants to piss us off. But if this system actually worked, it would help us all to thrive. It would bring everyone together instead of creating divisions."

Liv was almost certain that Clark was going to roll his

eyes at her after this monologue, so she was surprised when he simply smiled.

"If you ever have a chance, repeat those words verbatim at a meeting with the Seven," Clark stated. "I have a feeling that's exactly what many are thinking but are unable to voice."

"But why?" Liv questioned. "Why doesn't anyone stand up for anything around here?"

"I don't know," Clark said, appearing defeated. "Because it's hard. Because we don't want to create friction or be cast out. Because those who do are punished. Because it doesn't do any good."

Liv fumed, her fury making her ears hot. "That's such bullshit."

"I agree," Clark said, pulling out a book. "But you don't seem to care about any of that."

"Why would I care if I pissed off Adler?" Liv challenged.

"Because then he will find a way to assign you deadly cases," Clark explained. "Who knows what else he's got in the works for you? All I know is that those who opposed him in the past didn't do it for long."

Liv was about to protest when Clark's eyes widened as he read through the book in his hand. "I think this is it."

Liv grabbed the book out of his hands, scanning the page he had opened. "You're right, this explains about the garden."

Clark pointed to halfway down the page. "More importantly, there's information on the fountain."

"A mermaid?" Liv said with disbelief, reading. *"That's* what in the fountain? How is that even possible?"

Clark pressed into her, trying to read the book over her

shoulder. "Because look, the fountain isn't as shallow as it appears to be."

Liv knew that from the one time she'd accidentally fallen in there. She had sunk for what felt like a long time before her father pulled her out. "It's thirty feet deep! How am I supposed to find the thing that Rudolf wants?"

Clark who had obviously skimmed the entire page already, pointed to the sentence at the bottom of the page. "It should be easy to find it."

Liv's eyes ran over the place where he indicated and read, "The mermaid guards only one thing."

"So you just have to find out what she's guarding and take that," Clark said matter-of-factly.

"Yes, while I'm breathing underwater," Liv joked. "That sounds totally easy."

"It's a mermaid," Clark reasoned. "They are sweet, and sing songs to sailors. How hard can this be?"

"If it wasn't hard, Rudolf would have done it himself," Liv reasoned.

Clark shook his head. "No, because he can't come into the House of Seven. He needs you to do it. So you dive into the fountain, take what the mermaid is swimming around, and then you get out of there."

Liv gave him an uncertain expression. "Something tells me it's not going to be that easy."

Clark shrugged. "Want to search for a book on mermaids?"

Liv shook her head. "I actually already have a book that will tell me a lot."

"Oh, *Mysterious Creatures*," Clark guessed. "Yeah, I'm

sure that will have some useful information. Let's see what it says."

Liv pushed the volume about the gardens in the House of Seven into Clark's hands and withdrew *Mysterious Creatures* from her robe. She was unsurprised when the small book opened to the chapter on mermaids. The image on the next page nearly made her drop the book. Even though it was only an illustration, for a moment it appeared real enough to jump off the page for some reason.

The mermaids depicted in the book didn't have a sweet smile and beautiful hair cascading over her shoulders. Mermaids were ugly, with seaweed hair, large squinty eyes, and sharp teeth and claws.

"That's a mermaid?" Clark asked, again reading over Liv's shoulder.

"Yeah, and she doesn't look like a reasonable creature I can simply negotiate with," Liv stated.

"No, she looks hungry."

Liv slapped the book shut, having read the short description on mermaids and found it not entirely helpful. Knowing that they preferred cold salt water and small spaces didn't give her any great ideas about how to deal with the creature. Their hunting and sleeping patterns would have been slightly useful, except Liv knew right away she wasn't dealing with a regular mermaid. Most were found in the ocean, but this one was confined to a solitary tank, seemingly designed for it.

"What are you going to do?" Clark asked, reading the determination on her face.

"I'm going to get help from an expert."

CHAPTER TWENTY-SEVEN

"If you know anything about mermaids, tell me now and save us the trouble of this trip," Liv encouraged Plato as they approached Rory's house.

"I know that they don't share very well, and prefer young men over older ones," he stated.

"I don't think that tidbit of knowledge is as helpful as you may believe," Liv said.

"I once spent some time on a boat that sailed into mermaid-infested waters," Plato explained, strolling beside her with his tail high in the air.

"What happened?"

"I survived," Plato answered simply.

"Shocking. Thanks for the spoiler alert. And what about the passengers and crew aboard?"

"They lasted longer than I would have expected," Plato explained. "We floated into dense fog, and by the time we came out on the other side, the ship was quickly sinking to the bottom of the ocean."

"You didn't learn much about mermaids from that, I gather."

"I learned that those who stand by the edge of the ship go overboard first. And I also learned that almost everyone goes overboard eventually."

"Thanks, but I think I'm going to need more information." Liv stopped, eyeing Plato. "This ship you were on… Would I have heard of it?"

Plato's eyes slid to the side.

"Was this the *Titanic*?" Liv asked.

Right on cue, Plato disappeared. Once again, Liv assumed it was her question, but she also noticed that the kittens were playing in Rory's yard. She laughed to herself. "Okay, I'll take that as a yes, Plato. And here everyone thought it was an iceberg that took down the ocean liner."

She was pretty sure that Plato could rewrite the history books by himself.

The kittens all came charging to her feet when she stepped into the yard. She knew there was a magical fence that kept them in the yard since Junebug was always trying to escape. However, she'd never seen the other nine kittens in the front yard like this.

Leaning over, she scratched a few of the closest kittens on their heads while the others fought to get her attention. "What are you guys doing outside? Outgrowing the house, are you?"

A few of them meowed in response. Liv smiled at them before starting off again for the house. Strangely, the door didn't open in response to her presence. She knocked, expecting for the door to slide back and grant her entry. Liv waited a full minute before knocking again. When that went unanswered, she began to worry and tried the handle, which turned.

She pushed opened the door a crack, but the kittens pressed their heads against the door, pushing it open farther as they charged past her into the house.

"Rory?" Liv called, peeking into the living room. It was quiet, and even stranger, it was sparkling clean. Literally. Sparkles radiated off the dining room table and floors like they'd been polished for hours. When she took a step into the house, her boot made a squeaky noise.

"So *this* is squeaky-clean," Liv muttered to herself.

"And another thing," Bermuda's voice echoed from the kitchen. "Tomatoes go on the countertop, not in the refrigerator—not that you should be eating too much food from the nightshade family. You know it gives you gas."

"I know that, Mum," Rory groaned from somewhere in the house.

"And another thing—what are the kittens doing back in the house?!" Bermuda yelled.

Liv's eyes widened as the rest plowed through the open door. She bent over, grabbing up a handful of them, their little claws scratching her forearm as they tried to escape. She was about to put them out the door when thunderous footsteps advanced in her direction.

Bermuda came around the corner of the dining room as Liv straightened, holding three kittens in her clutches, the rest having sought refuge under the sofa.

"What have you done?" Bermuda yelled, her round face red with frustration. "I just cleaned this place, and those little mess-makers have already tracked dirt all over the house again."

Liv backed up to the floor mat in front of the door, holding the kittens tighter, sort of afraid for her life as she stared up at the red-faced giant.

"And you!" Bermuda continued. "Were you raised in a barn? You've still got your boots on inside the house. Don't you know any better, child?!"

Liv tried to open the door with her elbows as she worked to take off one boot using her opposite heel. The visual had to be ridiculous, she thought, but the menacing look Bermuda was giving her couldn't be ignored. Liv had faced demons and giant snakes and many other monsters, but none of them inspired the fear in her that Bermuda did.

"I'm s-s-sorry," Liv stuttered, one of the kittens sidling from her grasp and sprinting for the back bedroom.

Bermuda simply stared at her, her lips forming a hard line.

"I'll clean it up," Liv continued. When she got the door open, the other two kittens leaped from her arms, scrambling madly for the kitchen. Not deterred, Liv pulled off her boots, smiling broadly as she turned around to face the giant. Her eyes followed Bermuda's, and she quickly realized the damage had already been done. A huge clump of dirt sat a few feet from the mat, looking like the biggest piece of debris in the world on the pristine floor.

"What's going on?" Rory asked, striding into the living room from the back. Junebug was on his shoulder. The kitten sprang free, dropping onto the couch, where he wrestled with pillows, making a mess of the furniture.

Liv couldn't stop the laugh that burst from her mouth at the sight of the giant. His usually chaotic curly hair was neatly parted down the middle and slicked back. Even stranger, he was wearing a starched white shirt buttoned all the way to his neck, and suspenders and khakis and loafers.

He rolled his eyes and dropped his hands to his sides, exasperated. "Oh, no, you didn't."

"She did," Bermuda said, tapping her foot impatiently.

"I'm sorry… I didn't… I'll clean up the mess I made," Liv said, raising her hand.

Bermuda shook her head. "Oh, no, you don't. Your brand of magic will only make things look worse. Magicians are the worst with cleaning spells."

Liv's eyes darted to Rory for help. He shook his head minutely.

"Actually, I think that goblins are worst housekeepers," Liv said. "They literally sweep everything under the rug with their magic, which ironically doesn't work very well since they don't *have* rugs, so all the dirt ends up piled up in the middle of the floors of their huts."

Rory sighed deeply.

Bermuda nodded at her son. "I agree, your apprentice doesn't know when to be quiet."

"Apprentice?" Liv questioned.

"It's a problem that magicians have," Bermuda continued. "They like to hear themselves talk, although they should spend more time listening if they are ever going to be of any use to this planet."

The room fell silent, except for the sound of the kittens burrowing inside the sofa.

"So those are some nice suspenders," Liv teased Rory.

"Don't," he snapped.

"They *are* nice," Bermuda said, glancing proudly at her son. "Doesn't he look handsome?"

"Ummm—"

"Actually, don't answer that. I don't want to hear what you think of my son," Bermuda cut her off, returning her attention to her son. "Maybe you should go and work on the chicken coop in the back, Ro."

"You're getting chickens?" Liv asked. "Won't the kittens be a problem for them?"

"Not if they live outside in the front where cats belong," Bermuda replied.

Rory scratched his shoulders and fussed with his clothes.

"Now, don't do that. You'll mess up your suspenders," Bermuda scolded, circling her finger and drawing the kittens out of the sofa. Their claws tried to grip the floor as a magical force pulled them to the door.

"I don't like the suspenders," Rory grumbled.

"And yet, they keep your pants on your buttocks." Bermuda forced the kittens out the door with a swipe of her finger, closing the door with a swoosh.

"Buttocks," Liv repeated with a giggle, earning a frown from Bermuda.

"Is there a reason you're here, magician?"

Liv couldn't help herself, although she was admittedly not trying very hard to control her responses. She said, "Besides to see Rory pull the wedgie out of his tight pants?"

He closed his eyes as if hoping to transport himself to another dimension. He'd probably choose one with demons and fire-breathing dragons at this point.

"Do not think that I've so soon forgotten that you

insulted me in the village of the giants," Bermuda said to Liv.

This made Rory whip his eyes open. "Liv? You did what?"

Liv blinked, trying to remember what Bermuda was talking about.

Crossing her thick arms over her chest, Bermuda said, "You told me in front of my tribe that my old age hadn't made me any more attractive."

Rory stuck both his hands into his hair, pulling it loose from the gel.

"Oh, no, you didn't."

"I was pretending to be Decar Sinclair," Liv explained. "I obviously didn't mean it, but rather was trying to stay in character. Isn't that something that Decar would have said to you?"

"Quite possibly," Bermuda agreed, throwing her nose in the air and still looking offended.

"Well, I apologize if I offended you," Liv stated. "I, of course, think you're as beautiful as a spring rose."

That was apparently not the right thing to say. Bermuda gestured in Liv's direction as she glared at her son. "You see the disrespect that magicians show to us? The offenses never stop."

"Wait, I meant that as a compliment," Liv argued.

The three fell silent, Bermuda glaring at Liv, Rory staring at the floor like he was hoping to fall through it, and Liv teetering back and forth, wondering how to break the tension.

"Roses are considered one of the most unattractive flowers among giants," Rory informed her.

"Of course they are," Liv said dryly.

The uncomfortable silence between the three grew.

"Soooo…" Liv said, drawing out the word. "Is this a good time to ask you for help, Mrs. Laurens? I have a situation that could use your expertise."

Bermuda threw up her hands, sighing deeply. "Of course she needs my help."

"It's really important," Liv stated. "I mean, you don't have to offer me any help, but if you don't, I'll be a fae's servant for ten years, which will sort of stop our progress on that whole 'finding the truth' business. Your call."

"Fine!" Bermuda said, thundering into the kitchen.

"Fine as in I should leave?" Liv called after the woman.

"Fine, as in I'll help you," Bermuda answered, her voice shrill.

"Oh, well, should I follow you?" Liv asked, looking at Rory, who refused to glance up from the floor.

"No!" Bermuda yelled. "I'm getting you crumpets, fruit, and some duck sausage. Otherwise, I fear you'll waste away in front of me. Seriously, it's hard to look at you without feeling your hunger pangs."

"Thank you?" Liv said, uncertainty in her voice.

Rory glanced at her now, shame written on his face.

"So, you and Mum having fun catching up?" Liv dared to ask.

He narrowed his eyes at her. "Yes, and thanks so much for suggesting that she come and live with me while we investigate."

"You're… you're welcome," Liv said, believing that Rory was close to murdering her.

"She told me about my pops," Rory said in a low voice.

"And the secrets that she kept hidden?" Liv asked.

He nodded. Swallowed. "I guess I should be thanking you. I wouldn't have known any of this or that this secret was this big, affecting the giants, if not for you."

Liv didn't know what to say to that. It was rare for Rory to show her any gratitude. "Your hair is…"

"Don't." He shook his head, which broke his curls free of the gel.

"You lot get over here and eat up before it gets cold," Bermuda ordered.

Liv gave Rory an uncertain expression, but he ushered her forward. "Go on. I can't wait to find out what you need her help with."

"Oh, I think you *can* wait, but I like your attempt at sarcasm," Liv said over her shoulder to him as Bermuda brought a huge tray into the living room.

When she set it down, Liv didn't think she'd ever seen such a compelling spread in all her life. China plates were piled high with fluffy crumpets surrounded by jars of homemade jam. Mounds of artfully arranged fruits sat in beautiful blue bowls decorated with little white daisies, and still steaming were a stack of sausages, the smell of which had the kittens scratching at the door. There was enough food on that one tray to feed Liv for days.

"Don't you have anything to eat?" Liv asked, halting in front of the table, which was covered with a lacy cloth and set with pink and white chinaware.

"Sit and eat, magician," Bermuda ordered, not appreciating her attempt at sarcasm.

To Liv's relief, a smile sort of cracked Rory's face when she glanced at him. He urged her to the chair beside him.

"So, the thing is—"

"I said eat," Bermuda reprimanded her, handing the plate of sausage to Liv. She pursed her lips and looked at Rory. "Magicians are the worst listeners. In all my dealings, they hear what they want to hear and ignore anything else."

Liv buttoned her mouth shut, taking a sausage from the plate and handing it to Rory with a tense expression. He seemed to be urging her to remain quiet, but they both knew that wasn't going to last long.

Bermuda piled a dozen small round crumpets on Liv's plate.

"Thanks, but that's probably more than I need—"

"Eat them," Bermuda ordered, cutting her off.

"Although I appreciate the spread, I just had lunch and—"

"Ro, did I make myself completely clear to your magician friend? She doesn't seem to understand me."

"Thing is, I'm an adult, and I don't do what other people tell me to, even when I need their help," Liv said, pushing her plate away.

Bermuda grabbed the perfectly pressed pink napkin in her hand, crushing it. "Magicians have no idea how to be civil."

Liv couldn't stand it anymore. She stood abruptly from the table, still not as tall as the seated giants. "Will you please tell me something else that magicians do wrong? I really love getting this education from you."

Bermuda's face pinched with hostility.

"Ro, are you going to allow your guest to speak to me like this?"

Rory looked between his mum and Liv, like he was

trying to decide. Then he shrugged. "Yeah, I think I am. There is really no controlling Liv."

Bermuda picked up her napkin and threw it on the table, her anger palpable. "That's it, Ro! Go out and work on the chicken coop. I'm going to have a word with this runt magician."

Rory let out a heavy sigh. "No."

Bermuda flinched. "What did you just say to me, son?"

"I said, no," Rory stated simply.

Bermuda gave Liv a murderous expression, her face vibrating with anger. "Get out of here, magician!"

Rory stood beside Liv. "No, Mum."

Bermuda looked at her son and Liv, confused outrage in her eyes. "What is going on here?"

Liv took a step backward, hoping to hide behind Rory if necessary.

"I don't want to build a chicken coop," Rory began. "I like my yard the way it is, and I buy eggs from Mrs. Anderson at the Farmers' Market."

"But she's a mortal," Bermuda complained. "I saw those eggs. They were small compared to the ones you *could* have."

"They work just fine," Rory said matter-of-factly. "And I like supporting her, because she's a nice lady."

"But she's—"

"Yes, she's a mortal," Rory cut in. "You used to have more tolerance for mortals and others."

"I think that your time living away from the village has colored your view," Bermuda remarked.

Rory shook his head. "No, it hasn't. If anything, I see things more clearly. I understand what Liv wants, and she's right that we can't keep living with so many divisions, which means you shouldn't treat her like she does everything wrong."

Bermuda's mouth popped open, but she didn't say anything.

"And another thing," Rory said, taking down the suspenders, "I don't like these clothes. While I appreciate your input, I like the clothes I usually wear and the way I wear my hair."

He then pointed at the door, making it fly open. The kittens sprang into the living room from outside, led by Junebug. "And I like my kittens in the house."

"But they are—"

Rory held up his hand, cutting off his mother. "Yes, they are mess-makers, but I don't mind that so much. This is my house, and while you're welcome to stay here always, you must respect the way I live." He clapped a hand on Liv's back, nearly knocking her into the table. "And you have to respect my friends."

Once Liv had recovered from coughing up a lung, she looked up proudly at Rory. He didn't return the smile she gave him.

"Well, I didn't realize I was exerting so much of my influence on your life, Ro," Bermuda said, looking around the table indecisively. After a moment, she managed a smile. "Can we try again? I'll try to remember your boundaries. I guess it's hard for me not to take over when it comes to house and family things."

Rory nodded, pulling out Liv's chair and offering it to her. She tentatively took a seat, peeking at Bermuda as she did.

The giant studied Liv, pressing her lips together. She picked up a new napkin from the side of the table and folded it into her lap. "Well, shall we eat?" She shut her mouth suddenly and sat back in her seat. "I meant to say, there is food if you are hungry." She grabbed a crumpet and spread jam on it, apparently trying to quell her emotions.

Liv gave Rory a sideways glance as he took a seat next to her. "This looks great. Thank you, Mrs. Laurens."

"Now, you had a question for me? Go on." Bermuda took a small, proper bite of the tiny crumpet.

"Right, yes," Liv said, trying to compose herself after the strange conflict. "I was wondering if you could tell me how to get past a mermaid."

As civilized as Bermuda was trying to be, she choked on her bite, the half-chewed food flying across the table and landing in front of Liv's plate.

She eyed it and then Rory before looking at Bermuda. "So, this is going to be a piece of cake then, huh?"

CHAPTER TWENTY-EIGHT

Liv pushed her plate forward, covering the half-chewed bite sitting before her on the table.

Bermuda dabbed the corners of her mouth. "Now, dear, I appear to have misheard you. I could have sworn you said something about mermaids. What did you really mean?"

Liv nodded. "I meant mermaids."

Rory pushed away from the table, covering his forehead with his hands.

Liv ignored him, focusing her attention on the giant on the other side of the table. "I read the section of your book about mermaids, Mrs. Laurens, but I didn't find any strategies for getting by them. And actually what I need is to get something away from the mermaid."

Apparently having lost her appetite, Bermuda slid her plate away. "No one in their right mind would try to get past a mermaid or take what they are guarding from them."

Liv laughed. "That's par for the course for me."

"Mag—" Catching the glare Rory flashed her, Bermuda changed her approach. "Liv, this is quite serious. Mermaids have the prowess of the worst sea monsters. Sharks and whales have nothing on them. But to make it worse, they have the cunning of the most seductive and deadly women on Earth. I didn't offer any strategies in my book for dealing with them because there are none."

Liv deflated with defeat. "Well, I have to try something. I can't just give up."

Rory tapped his fingers on the table, the wheels turning in his head. "This is what you have to do for Rudolf?"

Liv nodded. "The mermaid is in the fountain in the House of Seven's garden. I don't know what she's guarding, but she has to have been there for a long time."

Bermuda, looking uneasy, reached for her teacup. "I fear that whatever she's guarding is going to complicate things even more."

"Knowing Rudolf, it's a gem or a watch or some other strange treasure," Liv stated.

Bermuda blew on her hot tea. "I'm not so sure. Mermaids are really only interested in one thing, and they will kill anything that tries to take it from them."

Liv leaned forward and Rory did the same, both of them highly curious about what Bermuda would say.

She set her teacup down. "Well, isn't it obvious?"

Liv and Rory glanced at each other, their faces full of confusion.

"It isn't to me," Liv said. "How about you, Ro?"

He rolled his eyes at her but shook his head. "Yeah, I have no idea."

Bermuda dropped two lumps of sugar into her tea. "It's mortals. Mermaids are obsessed with mortals. They only go after vessels that have mortals aboard. They'll murder a magician or any other magical creature who gets between them and their feast."

"Wait, then that means that mermaids want to eat mortals, but this one is apparently guarding something else because a mortal wouldn't be alive at the bottom of the fountain," Liv reasoned.

Bermuda nodded as she stirred her tea. "I agree, which means the mortal isn't alive. That makes the most sense, because mermaids only eat their prey alive."

"So the mermaid is guarding a bunch of bones?" Liv asked.

Bermuda looked at her son. "She *does* understand how magic works, right?"

"Barely," he answered with a sigh.

"Hey, there," Liv warned. "I'm learning. I don't have the benefit of your many, many years on this Earth, old man."

Again he rolled his eyes at her.

"Liv, if the mermaid is in fact guarding something, then it must be a mortal, probably in a preserved state," Bermuda said, trying to take another sip of her tea. "She might be waiting for the mortal to awake. Mermaids, as deceptive as they are, aren't the brightest. They tend to fantasize and pine for things they can't have."

"Well, then I just have to offer her something that she'll like more than guarding a dead mortal," Liv reasoned.

Bermuda clapped, the action sounding like a fire-cracker going off. "That's actually good. You can bait her with a different mortal. Do you have one you can throw to her?"

Liv shivered with disgust. "No! That's horrible. And no. Just no."

"Well, you need a way to distract the mermaid, and she's going to be hungry," Bermuda said.

"Not to mention dangerous," Rory imparted.

"Yes, and the fact that you can't breathe underwater will be another disadvantage for you," Bermuda said.

Liv let out a heavy sigh. "Why can't I just drain the damn fountain and watch as the beast flops around while I get the prize?"

Bermuda gasped with shock. "For starters, mermaids are endangered species. If you killed her, I'd be liable to report you to the Threatened Magical Creatures office."

"Of course you would," Liv said dryly. "Didn't you just say that it was impossible to get past a mermaid? Why are they dying out?"

Bermuda shrugged. "Because, like I said, they aren't smart. They end up in fishing traps or tangled up in trash in the ocean. Usually they see the nets as some sort of oasis."

"Okay, so I have to get into the fountain, get past the mermaid, and retrieve a mortal's body, which, by the way, I have no idea what it's doing in the House of Seven," Liv said.

"Stay focused on the problem at hand," Bermuda commanded. "It's none of your business what the body is doing there, but using a minimizing spell will help with carrying it to the surface."

"Can I try to bait the mermaid with something else?" Liv asked.

"Only mortal blood will be of interest to her," Bermuda answered. "However, the moment you slip into that fountain, she'll attack you to defend her mortal."

"Would a disguising spell work?" Rory asked.

Bermuda shook her head, taking another bite of the crumpet she had tried to eat before. "They can't be fooled like that due to their sense of smell."

Liv stood suddenly, an idea occurring to her out of nowhere. "But her sense of hearing would work the same way as other sea creatures', wouldn't it?"

Bermuda appeared perplexed. "Well, yes…"

"Then I think I have an idea that could work, but I need to get to John's shop first." Liv grabbed a crumpet and waved to the two giants. "Thank you for all your help!"

CHAPTER TWENTY-NINE

The placid waters of the fountain reflected Liv's image. She stared into the pool, seeing shimmering blues and greens deep in the water.

She glanced down at Plato beside her. "What do you think of the plan?"

"I think it could work," he answered, his eyes on the water. "But it could also not work."

"I knew you were going to say that."

"Then why ask the question?" Plato said.

"Well, it's this thing people do when they need to be reassured and encouraged in a dangerous situation," Liv answered.

Plato plastered a fake grin on his face, which looked all wrong, as if he were a deranged cousin of the Cheshire Cat. "You can do this. Go, you."

Liv grimaced. "Don't ever be cheerful again. It doesn't suit you."

His smile dropped. "I could have told you that."

Liv pulled the Fish Finder that Mr. Simmons had

dropped off at the shop for her to fix from her pocket. She'd repaired it but had conveniently forgotten to tell him that it was ready for pickup. She'd return it to him after one small use. Turning the device on, she waited for the sonar sensor to detect whatever was in the pool. A moment later, it showed a giant fish on the far-right side of the fountain.

"Looks like we found our pretty lady," Liv said, striding to the opposite side of the fountain, some twenty yards away.

"Yes, I'm sure she's pretty. About like an anglerfish," Plato stated.

Pulling off her cape and boots, Liv prepared for the plunge. She knew the water was going to be cold, and that she'd have to swim fast. What she didn't know was if the minimizing spell she'd just learned would work on the mortal's body so she could easily carry it to the surface. When she'd practiced it on the refrigerator in John's shop, it had made it so that it was lighter but not any less bulky. Plato had stated that was how the spell was supposed to work. Too bad for Liv, she'd learned how to expand things, like the shop, but hadn't figured out how to do the opposite with a compacting spell.

Liv would have taken the time to learn the spell, but Plato informed her that they didn't work well on physical beings and could have permanent side effects. It would do no good to retrieve the mortal for Rudolf, only to deliver a tiny person who wasn't in the shape he wanted them.

"Why does Rudolf want some mortal who is sleeping at the bottom of the fountain in the House of Seven again?" Liv asked Plato.

The lynx flicked his tail, watching the surface of the water. "Dead," he corrected. "His mortal is dead, most assuredly. A sleeping spell wouldn't work underwater."

"Okay, same question as before," Liv said. "Why does he want some dead person?"

"Some people are into that," Plato said with a laugh.

"Oh, gross." Liv grimaced.

"I'm sure you'll find out when and if you're successful."

"Again, can we work on being a bit more positive when I'm about to risk my life for a mission?"

"Okay," Plato affirmed. "But do I have to be positive otherwise?"

Liv shook her head. "No. I realize that would kill your spirit, and I wouldn't want that."

After she'd rolled up her sleeves and removed her socks, Liv tied her hair back, trying to minimize anything that could potentially slow her down. It had been a lifetime since she had gone swimming. Many in Los Angeles went to Malibu or Santa Monica and swam on the weekends, but firstly, Liv didn't like the tourists who were always clogging up the beaches with their popup tents and bratty kids. And secondly, swimming in freezing-cold shark-infested water wasn't the least bit appealing to her.

She laughed at the irony as she stared at the chilly pool of water where a monster resided, guarding something that she couldn't leave without.

The vial of John's blood that Liv had taken from him was still warm thanks to the spell she'd put on it. She was a little tired of taking blood from people she loved, like when she'd had to use Sophia's to trick Queen Visa. However, Liv was pretty certain that she needed John's blood to make this work, and also, it was viable as bait to entice the mermaid as long as it was fresh. Liv hoped that the blood of a mortal was enticing enough to take the mermaid away from the spot she was guarding.

Finally, Liv pulled the sonar device she'd made from under her cape. This was the part of her plan she doubted the most. There had been no way to test it, and it was unique technology since she'd created it herself—after fixing the Fish Finder, of course. Using a normal active sonar device she'd found in the junk bin in the shop, Liv had tweaked it using magical tech. She wasn't sure if her skills were up to par for combining her magic with electronics, but all of her mess-ups fixing things had paved the way. Once she had repaired and upgraded the device, Liv had made it so that she could increase the frequency, which, when combined with the magic tech, would hopefully make the mermaid a non-issue.

Liv laid the device down beside her cape right in front of Plato. "You know what to do?" she asked him.

"I click that button on top," he answered, holding up his paw like he was going to do it right then.

"Do you know when to do it?" she grilled him.

He nodded. "When it's time."

Liv rolled her eyes. "Do you know when that time is?"

"Before you get eaten."

Liv shook her head. "If I die in this fountain, I will haunt you for the rest of your long-ass life."

"Good, you can join the club," Plato said seriously.

"And if someone comes into this area of the garden?" Liv quizzed.

"Then I disappear, leaving you to fend for yourself," Plato answered.

"I don't believe that was what we discussed."

Plato huffed with annoyance. "I'll use my voodoo to ensure I'm not seen, but otherwise, I'll be right here, monitoring the sonar device."

Liv wasn't sure how long the sonar device would work, but she was gambling on having at least a minute, or maybe a bit longer where the mermaid was no longer incapacitated. That was why the timing had to be right. And she wasn't sure it would work, but she was running out of time to experiment.

Uncorking the vial of blood, Liv offered Plato one last look, full of hesitation. "Okay, get ready. It's almost time."

"Get ready for what?" he asked through a long yawn.

Liv couldn't help but laugh. "That's the kind of morale boost I expect from you. Thanks."

She turned the vial over, spilling the contents into the fountain and staining the water red.

Something jerked under the surface, knocking into the side of the wall on the far side.

"Looks like Viperfish is awake," Liv said, tensing all over.

The water rippled as the mermaid swam under the surface, and the waves increased as a dark figure moved closer to the top. She wasn't to the halfway point of the tank when Liv jumped up on the rim bordering the fountain and sprinted along the side, then dove in. She sincerely hoped the pool was thirty feet deep because her body was arched. She really didn't want to dive into a shallow basin, but it was too late to worry about that now.

Her hands reached out in front of her as the night air whipped across her face. Although it had been many years, her dive was in form, her hands touching the surface of the water first followed by her arms, head, and body.

The cold was piercing, the water dark. Liv kicked hard, headed for the bottom of the tank. Not only was she confined by how long the sonar device would work, she also knew that in this cold tank she wouldn't be able to hold her breath for long. Already her lungs were pulsing with the urge to breathe. Liv kept her lips pressed tightly together and pushed harder to the bottom.

The darkness grew as she got farther. Liv doubted if she'd even be able to see the mortal's body down there when a shimmering light caught her attention ahead. Bubbles blurred her vision as she swam.

A scream pierced the water, echoing in Liv's head. The mermaid knew she was there.

CHAPTER THIRTY

Liv dared to look over her shoulder, but all she saw was a commotion on the other side of the tank. There were bubbles everywhere, like something was caught in a tornado. Soon it would be time for Plato to start the sonar.

Although the mermaid was apparently faster than a shark, it would still take her a little while to cross the tank, which was one of the reasons to bait her on the other side. Also, there was little chance of getting to the mortal with the mermaid resting right on top of it, or however she spent her time.

Kicking hard, Liv finally caught sight of the mortal lying at the bottom of the fountain. It was a woman wearing a white gown. Her long brown hair floated around her, partially obscuring her pale face. However, Liv could tell that she was stunning, her features balanced and her skin flawless even after all this time submerged.

Liv pointed a finger at the mortal, sending the minimizing spell at her. Her body rose off the floor of the tank slightly.

So far, so good, Liv thought, feeling victorious.

Then it happened again—the scream, this time closer. Liv whipped around, and bubbles were rushing in her direction. That was when Liv saw her.

Hey, pretty lady, Liv thought, momentarily wondering if ugliness could be a weapon.

The picture in *Mysterious Creatures* didn't do the mermaid justice. Her long, flowing seaweed-like hair spread all around her, its pointy locks twirling as she sped in Liv's direction. Her mouth, with its rows of knife-like teeth, was open. Her dark eyes resembled those of a fish, large and unblinking. Her long-clawed hands reaching in Liv's direction, her black dorsal fin propelling her faster than a motor on a boat.

Hell, she's supposed to be incapacitated, Liv thought urgently. Could she create a portal here if necessary? She didn't think so. She realized she was screwed when the mermaid collided with her like a torpedo.

The mermaid's clawed hands grabbed Liv's arms, piercing her skin and sending blood into the blue waters. Liv brought her leg around to kick the mermaid in the chest, which under other circumstances would have been totally rude since she wasn't wearing a top.

The assault didn't have any effect on the mermaid, who screamed in Liv's face, her voice somehow making Liv's teeth hurt from the vibration.

She tried to pull free, but the mermaid was impossibly strong.

Sit-ups, Liv thought morbidly as she fought for her life.

The mermaid spent endless hours at the bottom of the tank doing sit-ups and other strengthening exercises.

The mermaid's jaw came unhinged, her face splitting almost in half, making her look like a strange doll. Liv knew what came next: one bite, and she'd be dead. Nothing could survive an attack from something that size.

Air escaped Liv's lungs as she kicked and thrashed, doing everything she could think of to fight the mermaid. If she could just get away an inch or two, she could try a spell on the creature, although they hadn't found anything that would be instantly effective. Still, dying at the bottom of the fountain after a short fight had the worst potential.

The mermaid's eyes widened as she pulled Liv into her to chomp down on her shoulder. The monster was going to eat her heart out.

This was the end, Liv thought, continuing to fight the impossibly strong mermaid.

The grip on Liv's arms loosened and she jerked free, kicking backward as the mermaid let go, floating away, her head lolling to the side.

It had worked! Liv could hardly believe it! And not a moment too soon. The sonar must have taken longer than she'd calculated to work.

She didn't waste any more time, swimming back in the direction of the mortal. Liv knew she only had twenty or thirty seconds before she was out of air. Scooping up the woman's body, Liv sped toward the surface of the water, her lungs aching for oxygen. She nearly opened her mouth, allowing water to surge into her body.

Just a bit farther, Liv encouraged herself, seeing the light brighten as she neared. The girl's hair flowed into her face, partially obscuring her view. Each second was making it harder to kick, and Liv was losing momentum. Even when she got to the surface, she'd still have to get the woman out of the fountain. It seemed hopeless, but she didn't give up.

She slowed when the surface was only a few feet away, finding it impossible to continue to carry the woman all the way to the top. Her lungs burned.

Only two more feet.

The mermaid screamed at the bottom of the fountain.

Liv pushed harder. *I can't ever give up. Not now, not ever.*

One foot.

She felt the surge of water under her as the mermaid sped toward her.

She'd never get out of the tank and pull the mortal out before the mermaid got her.

When Liv broke the surface of the water, she took a giant breath, her lungs drinking in the air and welcoming it like a spring day after the longest winter.

She was about to push the woman's body over the side of the fountain when something like a lion's mouth gently picked the woman up by her gown, pulling her out of Liv's arms. She barely had a moment to register the strange vision or protest when something bit into her ankle.

Liv screamed, grabbed the side of the fountain, and held on for dear life as the mermaid tried to yank her back under.

Trying to kick the mermaid in the face, Liv screamed. "Plato! The sonar!"

The lion disappeared, having safely put the woman's body on the ground beside the fountain. Liv squeezed her eyes shut, trying to pull herself up as the mermaid clawed at her legs. The only thing that had saved her so far was that the bite wasn't that big. However, soon the monster would unhinge her jaw like she had before and then she'd be done.

Her hand slipped on the edge, and she was quickly tugged under the surface and towed to the bottom.

She clawed through the water, trying anything she could think of to get away. She turned around and pointed her hand at the mermaid, about to send a defensive strike at her. Then, as before, the mermaid released her, floating lifelessly away.

The sonar device had worked again! But it wouldn't last long, Liv knew.

With her injured legs, she kicked to the surface, grateful when her hands found the edge of the fountain. She hauled herself over the side, sliding down ungracefully and lying in a heap next to the dead woman, exhausted and grateful to still be alive.

Her eyes fluttered shut. She just needed a minute to rest.

CHAPTER THIRTY-ONE

S omething was grabbing her leg. Liv kicked, thinking the mermaid had crawled out of the fountain and was about to devour her and take back her mortal.

"It's okay," a familiar voice said, a comforting quality in his tone.

Liv battled with the urge to keep her eyes closed, sleep crashing down on her, and her lids opened to a blurry world. A dark figure crouched in front of her, and he was wrapping her wounds in bandages. At least that was what she was hoping he was doing.

Pushing to a sitting position, Liv forced her eyes to focus. Stefan Ludwig was taking care of the bite and scratches on her leg. Finally feeling the pain after the ordeal, she let out a soft moan.

"Is it bad?" she asked him.

He shook his head, his dark hair falling into his eyes. "No, just surface wounds. It could have been way worse."

Liv nodded and looked around as Stefan charged to the other side of the fountain, gathering up her stuff. Plato was nowhere in sight, but she couldn't shake the image of him as a large lion. He had been majestic and beautiful, and he had saved her. If he hadn't pulled the woman out of the fountain, Liv would have never been able to get her out. And without her? Well, Liv would have stayed in the fountain until it was over. Until she was dead.

Stefan strode back over, looking around as if trying to decide if they were forgetting something.

When had he shown up? Liv would have to find out. The timing had been good, but now she had some explaining to do.

"Quick question. Totally no big deal," Stefan asked, regarding Liv with a half-smile as he stood in front of her. "Why are you hanging out with a dead girl in the garden?"

Liv brought her chin over to regard the cold, wet corpse. "Because I have the worst friends in the world."

"Yeah, you do," he said, shaking his head as he ran his eyes over the mortal's face. She was even more beautiful out of the water, her eyes closed like she was simply sleeping. Stefan pulled off his cape and threw it over the body. "Need help transporting this? I'm thinking you don't want to hang out here any longer. Unless you *want* Adler or Bianca to find you and have to stick around for an interrogation."

Liv groaned as she stood up, realizing she was dripping wet and shivering from the cold. "That would be great, if you wouldn't mind."

"Hey, what are awful friends for?" Stefan pointed to the long bite marks on her arm, the ones he hadn't dressed yet. "Should I be concerned that you're going to turn into a demon?"

She laughed darkly, pulling a piece of loose material from her already-ripped shirt. "Nah. Maybe a mermaid, though."

Stefan heaved the dead girl's body onto his shoulder. "Mermaid, huh? Wow, I can't wait to hear *this* story."

"It's totally boring," Liv said, tying the material around her arm. Then she took the cape that Stefan had put by the side of the fountain, catching the strange ripple on the surface of the water. She could have sworn she'd seen the mermaid's face staring at her, but when she blinked to clear her vision, there was nothing there—only shadows. She put the devices in her pocket, letting out a heavy sigh.

"A dead mortal and a mermaid. Sounds like a real snooze-fest of a story." Stefan pointed first at the body of the girl, making her look like a large bushel of potatoes on his shoulder. Then he pointed at Liv, drying her instantly. "Hope you don't mind that I helped you with that. You look a little weak from your battle or whatever you were doing in the fountain."

"I decided to take a swim," she admitted.

"That you did," he said with a laugh. "Tell me about it as you lead the way. Where do you want me to take the dead girl?"

"To my apartment," Liv said, limping from her injuries.

"Of course, you do," Stefan said. "That's where I keep all my dead bodies too. In my apartment."

Liv nodded over her shoulder. "So you get it, then."

CHAPTER THIRTY-TWO

At Liv's direction, Stefan laid the still-sopping-wet girl on the couch in Liv's apartment, the one that doubled as her fold-out bed.

Note to self: I'm getting a new bed, Liv thought, pulling out her phone to message Rudolf. Now that he'd allowed it, she had access to his phone number through the magical network. Apparently, he had to block it using special magic because of his many stalkers.

Stefan dried himself with the same spell he'd used on Liv before pulling out his own phone.

Liv gave him a cautious look.

"I'm calling Hester," he said, pressing the phone to his face. "Your bites need to be treated."

Liv nodded, knowing she could trust the healer. She'd probably laugh, wondering how Liv had gotten bitten by a mermaid and also a lophos. She had some dumb luck, for sure.

A moment later, Stefan ended the call, giving Liv a curious glare.

"What?" she said, limping over to the chair in the corner.

"Go on and tell me your story," Stefan ordered, crossing his arms over his chest. She'd had trouble keeping up with him on the way over there, not only due to her injuries but also because he moved faster than humanly possible, easily leaving her behind.

"I don't know who the girl is," Liv explained, telling him about the ring and the favor.

Stefan clicked his tongue and shook his head when she was done. "Seriously, how do you get yourself into these situations?"

"It's a gift," she admitted.

"Or a curse," he joked as the door burst open.

Rudolf's face was white as he sprinted into her apartment, and his clothes were disheveled, as if he'd put them on in a hurry.

"Yeah, go ahead and come on in," Liv stated dryly.

Rudolf stared around, his eyes landing on the mortal lying on Liv's couch, dripping water on the hardwood floor.

"Dumbo, will you tell me why there is a dead girl lying on my sofa?" Liv asked Rudolf who dove to the floor on his knees, cradling the young woman's face in his hands.

"Because..." he said, checking her over like he was unaware that her heart wasn't beating and he wanted to know if she was okay.

Liv glanced at Stefan. "I told you. Worst friends ever."

"I'm lucky to count myself as one of those people," Stefan said proudly, giving her a conspiratorial smile.

"Hey. Rudolf," Liv said, trying to get the fae's attention.

He was busy muttering incoherent things to the dead woman. "I know you're busy having a conversation with the dead, but I sort of need to know why you had me retrieve this body from the fountain, especially because it nearly killed me."

Rudolf glanced up like he had just noticed that she was there. "Oh, hey. Can we have some privacy?"

Liv's eyes darted from side to side. "Ummm...if you haven't noticed, my apartment only has one room."

Rudolf shook his head. "That's fine. You can watch. I'll wipe your memory when I'm done."

Liv picked up Bellator, which was conveniently lying on the shelf where she'd left it. Even though she'd been weak moments prior, fire now shot through her veins, making her next movements as fast as Stefan's. The sword's point poked Rudolf's back, and he straightened.

"Please don't make me kill you after all this," Liv said.

He tensed and held up his hands in surrender. Glancing over his shoulder, he nodded. "Okay, fine. But who is that?" He indicated Stefan, who was sitting in the corner.

"Stefan the demon hunter, this is Rudolf, who is the bane of my existence. Rudolf, this is Stefan, the guy who helped me get the dead girl back to my apartment," Liv explained.

Rudolf waved casually at Stefan. "Pleased to meet you. If you wouldn't mind not telling anyone about this, that would be greatly appreciated."

Stefan smiled. "I have my own secrets, so I totally get it. Don't worry."

Liv cleared her throat. "So, although this introduction business is awesome and I'm close to starving to death, why don't you explain to me what this mortal woman was doing at the bottom of the fountain in the House of Seven."

Bellator's tip was still pointed in Rudolf's direction. He sighed.

"Her name is Serena," Rudolf said, combing her wet hair off her forehead. "On our wedding day, Queen Visa found out about us. I should have known she'd never allow me to be happy. We'd had our fling and she'd thrown me to the side, but she never lets anyone go. Decades later, I found Serena, and we fell madly in love."

Liv yawned, exhaustion taking over her body. "I've heard this story before."

Rudolf shook his head, knocking her sword away with more force than she expected. She lowered Bellator. "You haven't heard this story before because its new. I fell in love, I swear it."

"With an aging mortal?" Liv questioned.

"Yes, because that's the reason Queen Visa and I didn't work out," Rudolf confessed. "I've never been like the other fae, only wanting lust and sex. I always longed for the real deal. Romance and true love."

Liv laughed loudly, earning a shocked look from Stefan.

"Come on!" she said to him. "If you knew Rudolf, you'd get how ridiculous this is. He's sexually harassed me no fewer than two dozen times. He's the epitome of chauvinism."

"That's because that's how I'm expected to behave," Rudolf argued.

Liv gave him a look of disbelief.

"Okay, fine," he acquiesced. "It's also sort of fun. That repulsed look you give me in response is totally worth it.

But I do have a heart. I'm not like the other fae. I wanted a romance unlike any other, and then I found Serena, and we fell madly in love. And it wasn't like when other mortals fall for me. She saw me for what I was and loved me, not despite my faults, but because of them. Serena was my one true love."

"But then she fell into the fountain at the House of Seven?" Liv asked.

Rudolf shook his head. "This was back when other races were allowed in the House of Seven. Queen Visa showed up to our wedding and killed Serena on the spot, then she took her body with her to the House of Seven. They were having a party of sorts. When no one was looking, she submerged her in the fountain, knowing that a mermaid lived there and would protect her forevermore."

"And you couldn't get to her?" Stefan asked, echoing Liv's hesitation.

He shook his head. "I tried, but Queen Visa did something that would ensure I never got close to her again. She ruined the party, creating chaos all over the house, possessing magicians' children, and making a mockery of the affair. The House kicked all the fae out and closed their doors to us for eternity."

Liv nodded in understanding. "She knew that if your race was banished, you'd never get to the body again."

"Yes. It was thankfully preserved, but that would do me no good," Rudolf explained.

He then pulled the purple stone he'd stolen from Father Time from his pocket. The purple gem caught the light.

"What is that?" Liv asked, prepared to raise Bellator again.

He ran his eyes over the stone appreciatively. "It's a revival stone. Your mother, at Papa Creola's orders, stole this from me, along with any other artifacts related to changing time." Rudolf gave her a look that she could only perceive as earnest. It was strange on his face, but it got her attention. "I know you have reason not to trust me, but you have to understand that I needed your help. I never meant for you to be in danger. I'll do everything I can from this moment forward to protect you and help you with your mission."

Liv shook her head. "Oh, no. I don't want to enter into any more agreements with you, fae."

Rudolf's gaze fell to the floor. "This isn't an agreement, Liv Beaufont, Warrior for the House of Seven." When he looked up at her, his eyes were brimming with tears. "This is a promise, one I can't break without losing my life. That's a law among the fae. I thank you dearly for what you've done for me, and in repayment for everything you've sacrificed, I will lay down my own life to protect yours, if the need ever arises."

Liv wasn't sure if she could believe him. She didn't know what to say. But she was highly curious about what would happen next. She pointed to the stone. "What are you going to do with that?"

A victorious smile flicked to his face, sparkling in his eyes. "For that, words won't suffice. You'll simply have to watch."

CHAPTER THIRTY-THREE

Rudolf closed his eyes, running his thumb over the revival stone and muttering incantations that Liv couldn't make out. His other hand was wrapped around Serena's wrist, his fingers resting on her pulse.

Liv knew what he was trying to do because she was good at math and could add two and two together. However, she was already thinking ahead. When this didn't work, how would she deal with Rudolf? She could see by the look in his eyes that he really believed he was in love with this woman, and he'd gone to great lengths to bring her back. But Liv's father had been very clear about one thing when teaching her about magic: "It can't bring back the dead."

Magic could turn back time, kill, erase events, create riches, and win wars, but it couldn't undo death. There were certain laws that governed that, and Liv knew they couldn't be broken. But Rudolf obviously didn't.

After a full minute of muttering, Rudolf's eyes snapped open, and a smile sprang to his lips. "It's done."

The woman lay exactly as before: unmoving, her skin white as a sheet, her long hair dripping water on the floor.

Liv let out a sigh. "Hey, it's okay—"

Rudolf held up a hand, stopping her. "Don't ruin this moment for me, love."

Liv gave Stefan a tentative look. She wasn't the one who was going to ruin this for him. Life was going to.

The room fell silent as Rudolf locked his eyes on the woman. The only sound was the water dripping from her hair.

Drip. Drip. Drip.

Liv didn't know how long they were going to stay like that before the reality set in for Rudolf. She wanted to believe that he really loved this woman, but maybe he was only in love with the *idea* of her; of having that which he couldn't. One thing was certain—Queen Visa was a horrible person and should be stopped. She'd been allowed to reign for too long, murdering without consequence. Silently, Liv put that on her agenda for future missions: take down the fae queen.

Drip. Drip. Drip.

Liv's stomach rumbled. It had been a while since she'd eaten, and fighting the mermaid had taken most of her strength. The thought of the mermaid caused her wounds to ache. She'd need to clean them soon. Hopefully, mermaid bites weren't poisonous.

Liv was off in thought when Stefan's rustling brought her back to the present. He leaned forward suddenly, his eyes intently on Rudolf.

Turning back to face him, she noticed that the revival

stone had begun to glow, but a moment later it faded. The woman remained still.

As I suspected, there is no bringing back the dead, Liv thought.

To her surprise, the stone faded to black. Rudolf closed his fingers around it, and it crumbled to dust and fell through his fingers to the floor. She was so going to make him clean that mess up and then buy her a new couch later. Liv clapped down on her insensitivity and silently punished herself for being so rude. Rudolf was going to be devastated when this didn't work. Liv sighed.

I'll wait a few weeks before I bring up the couch, and I'll clean up the dust myself, she thought.

But what were they going to do with the body? she wondered. That was a new one for her. So far she hadn't had to dispose of bodies, which was a good thing. Stefan would probably have a good idea. Maybe they could use a depour so it wasn't tracked.

Stefan wrapped his hand around Liv's arm, tugging on her lightly. She glanced up from the floor, where she'd been regarding the tiny dust pile while absorbed in thought.

To her amazement, color was starting to fill Serena's face, her cheeks rosy. Her chest rose and fell as if she were breathing.

But that was impossible!

Liv's eyes darted to Stefan; shock was written on his face too. He started, then put his arm across Liv's chest and pushed her back to the wall as a protective measure.

He had the same concern as her. If the woman was moving, that meant she was a zombie. That was the only way the dead could move. She'd heard of such things, and knew that this kind of magic was forbidden. It perpetuated itself, spreading evil. She couldn't believe she'd been a part of this.

Damn, Rudolf was going to get her in serious trouble—not to mention that they were going to have to fight a zombie. Liv gripped Bellator, glancing sideways at Stefan. He nodded minutely, reading the expression in her eyes. Between the two of them, the zombie wouldn't last long, but it was going to be a hell of a battle, and when it was done, she'd need more than a new couch. The apartment would most likely be destroyed.

Stefan pulled his sword in such a swift movement that Liv didn't even notice it until he had it all the way out and was ready to strike.

Rudolf spun around at the sound of the sword leaving its sheath, alarm in his eyes. "No, it's fine. Don't worry."

"She's a zombie," Liv stated. "What have you done?"

Rudolf shook his head. "No. It's okay, I promise."

Liv pushed Stefan's protective arm away from her and took a step forward. "You can't bring back the dead."

Rudolf held up a finger, some of the dust from the stone still on his hand. "You can't bring someone back without trading a life."

Liv glanced at Stefan, his confusion mirroring hers.

"Papa Creola took the revival stone away from me for a reason," Rudolf explained. The woman on the couch continued to breathe calmly, as if she were merely sleeping. "It's powerful magic that messes with time and defies certain laws. However, what I've done is perfectly fine by most standards of magic. It is simply unorthodox."

Liv gestured at Serena. "You brought back the dead! There have to be consequences for that, Rudolf."

He smiled even broader. "There are. The only way to bring someone back is to trade a life for theirs."

As if cued by his words, Rudolf aged before their very eyes. Not a lot, but since Liv was staring at him directly, she noticed the lines around his mouth and eyes deepen slightly. A few white hairs streaked his blond hair.

"Rudolf, what have you done?" Liv asked with a gasp.

His blue eyes sparkled with satisfaction. "I traded part of my life for Serena's. That's how the revival stone works."

"It can really bring back the dead?" Stefan asked in amazement.

Rudolf nodded. "Yes, but only with an even trade."

"What will happen to you?" Liv asked, her voice shaky to her surprise.

"It's fine. I have enough life to spare. It only cost me a hundred years," he explained.

"But what will that mean for you?" Liv questioned, looking between Serena and Rudolf.

"That means that I have less time on this Earth, but more time with the person I love," he answered.

"Yes, but she will only have a mortal life," Liv argued.

Rudolf grabbed the woman's hand. "It doesn't matter. If I have a full life with Serena, it will be enough. If we only have fifty or sixty or seventy years together, it will be the best part of my long life, and I'll die a happy man."

"Rudolf, what if this doesn't work?" Liv asked, watching as Serena stayed quite still.

He shook his head, admonishing her with a single look. "You know what you need, Liv?"

"A new couch? Smarter friends? A cheeseburger?" she asked.

He grinned widely. "You need faith. When you lose all else, it will keep you afloat."

Liv slapped her hand to her forehead. "I think you've been reading too much poetry. Faith doesn't win wars or keep you alive. It's something those who are out of options rely on."

Rudolf didn't look the least bit deterred. "Faith holds the real magic in life. What we believe with our hearts can come true. Faith can break unbreakable laws. It can change everything. It can defy every single odd. However, this isn't a magic most can master or use because it takes real discipline. It requires you to believe in that which doesn't yet exist. That's not something that most can do, because they will look like fools if they fail. But the person who believes wholeheartedly in their dreams is the most courageous. Their power is truly unstoppable. When you believe in yourself and your dreams, you are a mysterious creature whom few will understand and no one will be able to conquer."

The moment Rudolf finished his sentence, Serena sucked in a giant breath and bolted upright. Her hand clapped to her chest as if she were trying to cradle the heart that had just restarted.

The woman's eyes snapped open. They were dark brown and stared without seeing while her chest rose and fell with her deep breaths.

Rudolf winked at Liv before lowering himself down beside the mortal and looking at her with kind eyes. "My dearest love."

Serena blinked, studying her arms and legs before bringing her attention to Rudolf. She didn't seem to recognize him for a moment, and then a tear trickled down her cheek, landing on her white gown. "You did the unspeakable, didn't you, Dolfus?"

He nodded as she cupped his face in her hands.

"But you shouldn't have—"

"It's already been done, my love," Rudolf interrupted, kissing her on the lips.

Liv diverted her eyes, feeling like she was intruding on their moment. However, this was more than an intimate moment. This was a lesson in laws. In magic. In the power of true love. Liv could live another century and not see something as incredible as this.

In a few short minutes, Rudolf had taught her something that was more powerful than all the spells in the entire world. He had shown her that the real power existed in desire. It conquered all, trumped everything. It was the fuse that lit the biggest fires. It was desire that supported one's faith, and those two things had brought back a woman from the dead for Rudolf. Suddenly, the impossible was possible.

CHAPTER THIRTY-FOUR

When Liv was certain the couple had finished kissing, she dared to look back, but to her surprise found them gone. She blinked at the large wet spot on her couch before looking around as if expecting them to be in the kitchen, on the other side of the bar, or on the fire escape. However, they had left. Silently and magically, Rudolf and Serena had disappeared, off to spend the time together that had been stolen from them.

In pure astonishment, Liv turned to Stefan, shaking her head at him. "Seriously, I thought he was a super-big jerk. I never expected that."

He laughed. "No, you didn't. I suspect that on some level you trusted him, or you wouldn't have helped him. But I will admit that you have the strangest friends of anyone I know."

"I'll remind you that you're on that list," she teased.

A knock at the door startled them both. Stefan moved around Liv before she could get to the door, pulling it open in a blur of movements. He let out a sigh of relief at the sight of Hester DeVries on the other side of the threshold.

"Thank you for coming so quickly," he said, leading her into the small apartment. "Liv was attacked by a mermaid."

Hester was wearing a maroon crushed velvet traveling cloak with the hood pulled over her spikey gray hair. She frowned at Liv.

"You do like to test my skills, don't you?"

Liv couldn't stop herself. She pointed at Stefan in accusation. "He does too!"

Hester laughed, reaching over and gripping Stefan's shoulder affectionately. "I'll discuss you and your changed state in a moment. For now, I want you, Liv, on the couch so I can access your wounds."

Liv eyed the couch a bit reluctantly. "Ummm. Can we do that on the floor?"

Hester's forehead wrinkled as she studied the couch and the puddle of water around it and the dust drifting around in it. "I'm not sure you should tell me what happened here."

"I'm not sure I could if I tried," Stefan joked, taking his seat in the corner again.

Liv settled herself on the floor, pulling up her pants legs to display the bandages that Stefan had wrapped her wounds in while they were in the garden.

"Do you have any symptoms? Chills? Cravings for seafood?" Hester asked, examining the bite on her leg.

She shook her head. "I'm not going to turn into a mermaid, am I?" Liv asked.

"No, that's not how it works," Hester said. "But their bites can be poisonous. However, lucky for you, I treated you with a heavy dose of anti-venom when you were attacked by the lophos, and it appears to still be in your system. It protected you from the mermaid's poison."

"Lucky me," Liv said, winking at Stefan.

"In all my years," Hester said, running her hands over Liv's legs and causing her body to warm up, "I've never met anyone who survived both a lophos and a mermaid bite, not to mention a single person who had experienced both."

"Go big or go home," Liv joked.

Hester gave her a cautious look. "I'd recommend staying home for a little while after this."

"Oh, will I need to rest?" Liv asked.

Hester shook her head. "I know better than to try to tell you to rest, Warrior Beaufont. I can't give you any details, but your next case is...well, we tried to oppose it. I'm sorry."

Stefan's armor made noise as he leaned forward. "What is it?"

Hester looked back at him. "I can't say."

"If Haro voted for it, then it's okay," Liv stated, glad that she understood him better now.

Hester's eyes filled with dread. "He didn't. He voted against it."

"Well, then you have won the vote, right?" Liv asked.

Hester leaned forward. "Raina voted against us."

Stefan suddenly stood. "She wouldn't have done that."

The sadness in the healer's eyes was unmistakable. "I'm sorry, Warrior Ludwig. It's true."

"But why would she vote with Adler?" Stefan asked heatedly.

Hester shook her head. "I don't know. It all happened

very suddenly. One moment I recognized her, and then something shifted. But whatever it was, it's gone now. After the vote, I'm sure my friend was back."

"Why didn't you contact me?" Stefan said, stress coating his voice. "I need to see her."

Hester held up a hand, stopping him. "You need to be careful." She looked at Liv and Stefan with a warning in her eyes. "We all do. None of us are safe. I know you know that's true, more so than before."

"He brainwashed her with a spell, didn't he?" Stefan accused.

"I don't know. Truly I don't," Hester said, unraveling the bandages on Liv's arm and grimacing at the long claw marks. "I slipped your sister a concoction that should keep it from happening again, but that will only work until he finds other means. Adler doesn't like losing control of the council or anything else, and he's feeling more and more threatened."

"So she voted in his favor and then he released her?" Stefan questioned.

"I think so," Hester answered.

Liv held her breath as Hester treated her wounds. When she could speak again, she said, "Stefan, it's going to be okay. We'll figure this out."

He shook his head. "No, it's not. None of us are safe."

"That's why I have to keep investigating," Liv said.

"It sounds like you've got another death mission ahead of you," Stefan said, defeat in his voice. "Let me go with you, whatever it is."

Hester protested first. "No, you can't go on this one, Warrior Ludwig."

Stefan shot her a confused look. "But we make a good team. Together we are unstoppable."

Hester actually smiled as the wounds on Liv's arm closed before their eyes. "I agree, you two do work well together. However, Liv won't need you for this one. She'll be better off on her own. You'll only be a distraction."

"Distraction?" Stefan asked.

Hester rose, done treating her. "Warrior Ludwig, I'm grateful that you conquered your demon, but you know what this means?"

"That I make an even better demon hunter because I can sense the monsters?" Stefan guessed.

"Yes, there is that," Hester answered. "But it also means that you've lost your objectivity. I saw the way you responded to the crow. Where Liv has to go would blind you with fury. There's no way you'd come out of that place with your sanity intact."

Stefan's face showed intense worry. "Where are they sending her?"

Hester gave Liv a confident expression. "A place she can handle." Her smile was genuine. "Just get some rest, my dear. You have my faith."

Liv grabbed the healer's hand and squeezed it as she remembered what Rudolf had said. "Thank you. That's one of the best compliments you could give me."

CHAPTER THIRTY-FIVE

"You're really racking up the IOUs," Stefan observed, striding beside her as they made their way down the road.

Liv lifted a single eyebrow in response. "I don't know what you mean."

"Well, *I'm* forever in debt to you, and now you've got the fae. Who else?"

"Oh, you're ridiculous," Liv said with a dismissive wave. "I only helped save you because I didn't want your family replaced with someone potentially more annoying."

Stefan laughed. "And the fae?"

"He cons me into these things. Who knows what bullshit he'll pull on me next?"

"For someone who enjoys pretending she doesn't like people very much, your behavior suggests the opposite."

"Tell anyone, and I'll deny it absolutely," Liv said, then added. "Actually, tell my secret, and I'll tell yours."

Stefan chuckled. "That seems fair. If I tell people that

you actually value the human race, you'll tell everyone that I'm part demon."

Liv nodded. "It's totally reasonable."

Stefan halted when they reached the intersection. "But you have nothing to worry about. I don't talk to anyone about Liv Beaufont, although you are quite the talk of the town."

"I am not."

"Oh, you are. I hear your name whispered on the streets."

"I'm not sure that's a good thing. I have many enemies," Liv stated.

"The very best always do."

"So, what Hester said about you losing your objectivity… What do you think about that?" Liv asked.

He sighed deeply. "I've been feeling it more and more. There's a new fire in my being. It wakes me up in the middle of the night, urging me to get up and fight the evil in the world. At any given moment, I can find the nearest thief in the act of stealing or a criminal assaulting the innocent. Whatever the demon left in me, it lets me find evil easily."

"That sounds exhausting."

He agreed with a nod. "But I'm trying to keep a positive perspective. I think it will turn me into the greatest demon hunter and vigilante in the world."

She huffed. "You just have to be the best, don't you?"

He created a portal on the other side of him. "We both know we're neck and neck for that title."

Liv created an identical portal, her face becoming serious. "Are you okay about Raina?"

He paused. "Yes. I mean, no. I don't know. Nothing feels safe in the House anymore. I don't even know how to combat it anymore."

"And do you feel where the evil is coming from when you're in the House?" she asked.

He shook his head. "No, for some reason I don't. But that only means that it's masked."

"Don't worry," Liv stated. "We're immune now from the brainwashing that Adler can do, thanks to Hester. And soon Clark will be too." She felt in her pocket for the concoction the healer had given her for her brother.

Stefan's eyes flicked to the portal at her back. "Wherever you're off to next, try to be careful."

"You know I can't make that promise."

He conceded with a nod. "Okay, well, until I find you in a precarious position, take care of yourself, Liv Beaufont."

"You do the same, Stefan Ludwig."

He took a step backward, fading into the portal.

Liv found herself staring at it long after it disappeared. She had a feeling that Stefan's story was only beginning. That Warrior was bound to do things that would make history. She just had to ensure that the history books told the real story going forward, which meant she had to find out what had been rewritten.

CHAPTER THIRTY-SIX

"What did he promise her?" Clark asked, striding beside Liv as they made their way across the library in the House of Seven.

"I don't know," Liv whispered.

Clark sighed. "Sophia said the giant promised to give her a pet of some sort. If it's something illegal, we're going to be in trouble."

Liv halted in front of her brother. "You get what we're doing, right? And you're worried that Rory is going to give Sophia a three-headed chinchilla? You *do* know how to put things into perspective, right?"

He rolled his eyes. "This is serious."

"It's not. Not in the big scheme of things," Liv argued. Rory had also suggested to Liv that he wanted to take her to a special place. That was apparently where they'd get the gift he wanted to give Sophia. How could Liv argue with that?

His mother had set off on an adventure where she hoped to find more information on the "truth." With his mother gone, his spirits were higher than ever, and he'd stated that before Liv's next mission she should take a break and go with him to this faraway land. When she pestered him for details, he threatened to cancel the whole thing, which quickly shut her up.

"Can you tell me about this new death mission the council has in store for me?" Liv asked Clark.

His eyes darkened. "I'm sorry, but my oath prevents me from doing so."

"Hester appeared pretty upset about it," Liv supplied.

He nodded. "I think it was mostly the Raina thing, but I'm grateful it won't be happening again. At least not to one of us."

They both fell silent.

Liv was startled when her brother set his hand on her shoulder. "Don't worry, though. You've faced worse than this. Adler must be getting desperate, or he wouldn't resort to such extreme measures."

"But if he's getting desperate, that means he's onto us. You know what happens when he suspects people," Liv said urgently.

Clark shook his head. "No, he's onto *you*. You've created a rift in the House, and he knows it. He's losing his footing. There are more arguments among the council than ever before. Your rebellious attitude is infectious, and Adler is worried. However, I don't think he has any reason to believe you're anything more than a pain in his ass. Still, he doesn't want any conflict."

"Adler wants complete control, but that's not how the House of Seven was supposed to operate," Liv argued. "It was always supposed to be about balance between the families, not one man's agenda that trumped everything else."

"And then Liv came along." Clark offered her a proud smile. "I will be eternally sad that we lost Ian and Reese, but I can't tell you how happy I am that you're back. When you came back into my life, a light that was extinguished the moment you left flickered back on. You've changed everything. I'm not sure why I didn't come after you sooner and drag you back."

Liv grinned, swallowing the tenderness in her throat. "Because you knew I would have punched you in the face."

Clark pulled her into a sudden hug, pressing her in tight. "You would have, but I should have done it anyway. I should have never let you get away."

Liv pushed back, offering her brother a slight smile. "But me being away from the House was important."

"I know, but I hope it's never necessary again."

She hugged him again, talking into his shoulder. "No, it won't be. *Familia est sempiternum.*"

"Yes, *familia est sempiternum.*"

Liv released Clark in a swift movement and strode toward the wall with the symbols in the library. "Ready for this?"

Clark cleared his throat as he ran to catch up with her. "Oh, is it all business now?"

She winked at him. "You know it."

"I'm ready," he said when they stopped in front of the wall with the ancient language that danced around like it was excited for them to read its hidden meaning. For once, the area was empty. She'd told Stefan to stay away, and he'd agreed a bit reluctantly.

"Are you prepared for what we'll find?" Liv asked. "We may not like it."

Clark released a breath. "I'm almost certain we won't, but I promise that whatever it is, I'll help you defend it. Whatever it takes."

Liv nodded, tired of empty words. Action was what they needed now. She withdrew her mother's ring from her pocket and slid it onto her finger. She wasn't sure why, but that seemed like the thing to do. When the ring was in place, she felt a jolt that rocked her to her core.

Her vision went black, and then she saw her mother's face swimming in her vision: Guinevere when she was younger. When she married Theodore Beaufont. When she was initiated into the House of Seven as a Warrior. Her standing over an enemy she'd slain. Her holding Ian on the day he was born. Her as a mother to five children, checking on them as they slept in their beds before she left on the last day she was alive. Guinevere had walked out the door of their residence with her husband with this ring on her finger. She had then returned a moment later and slipped the Warrior ring off her finger. She had kissed it and then set it in a box on the table next to the door. "In case you'll ever need to find the truth. In case we fail. This is for you, my loves," she whispered and closed the box, sealing it shut with a spell only a Beaufont could open.

Liv gasped.

"What?" Clark asked, concern on his face.

She shook her head. "She was an amazing woman. She loved us more than life itself."

Clark gripped her hand. "You feel her?"

Liv nodded.

"I get those flashes with Dad, too. It's your connection to her as a Warrior."

Liv could hardly breathe. It was a sick joke. She felt her mother's presence so completely she could swear her arms were around her, and her words were beating in her head, telling her she could do anything. "Go forward, my child. Find the truth that lays before you. This is your destiny."

Liv pulled her hand from Clark's, fitting the Warrior's ring into the groove in the wall. She gave him a curt nod. "Your turn, bro."

His reluctant eyes communicated his fear, but he pulled the knife from his pocket. It had belonged to their father, and their family crest was etched on the hilt. He withdrew the blade, and before he could go back on things, he brought it across the palm of his hand, spilling his blood on the threshold between the library and the Ancient Chamber.

At least Liv wanted to believe this was the Ancient Chamber. Otherwise, she wasn't sure what this was, or whether it was supposed to be open.

The floor rumbled under their feet.

Liv pulled her hand away from the wall as dust rained down on them and Clark yanked her back, his blood-stained hand gripping her cloak.

They exchanged nervous glances, but a moment later their questions were answered. The wall parted, creating a path into a dark chamber—one that contained all the secrets they yearned to learn.

CHAPTER THIRTY-SEVEN

The smell that spilled out of the Ancient Chamber was reminiscent of something, but Liv couldn't put her finger on it. She would have expected must or dust or other old smells, but this was different. It was like moss, and grass, and other things that reminded her of her childhood. For some reason, these smells filled Liv with hope and pride. It made her want to charge forward, unafraid of what she was about to find.

She grabbed Clark by the hand and pulled him forward. He didn't need much encouragement.

They moved together, taking each step as one. And in truth, that was how Warriors and Councilors were supposed to operate: as one entity that presided over different areas of the House. She'd seen the epitome of this with her parents while she was growing up. However, this was the first time she had felt it. Clark was her other half. He was the uptight version of her. The tense to her calm. The practical side to her spontaneity. And Liv was the passion to his reservation. She was the fire to his cool. They were one, two parts of a whole.

When they stepped into the darkness, the wall shut behind them suddenly, making them spin around. For a moment they were in complete darkness, and then torches lit around them one by one, illuminating a room much larger than she would have expected.

Suddenly Liv felt like she was in an Egyptian tomb, looking around at the oldest carvings in the world as she studied the walls. They were full of more symbols that danced, but none of them seemed to be of major importance to her, although she wasn't sure why.

Liv wasn't sure what she had been expecting when they entered this area. It wasn't lavish or full of gems or glittering with golds and riches. This wasn't beautiful like the hallway in the entry to the House of Seven. It was dark and mysterious, but for some reason, she felt like she'd been here a million times. Maybe in her dreams? And then there were those smells… They were full of nostalgia and it pushed her forward, triggering a voice that said, "You're safe. Go on, my child."

Liv spun in a circle, trying to figure out what she was missing as she studied the domed room. It seemed to be telling her its secrets, but she wasn't sure she understood the message.

So she took another step, which made the torches grow brighter, illuminating more of the room. The area was similar to the Chamber of the Tree, except it was bigger. Different. And there was only one thing there she realized when they came to the middle of the circular area: a list of words in the ancient language, written in bold ink that glowed brighter than the torches.

She was about to step forward to decipher the words when the floor shook.

On the ground, blue and green spots like the ones in the Chamber of the Tree illuminated. However, there were more than seven. Like on her ring, fourteen spots shone.

They must represent the Warriors and the Councilors, she thought.

As if cued by her understanding, the tree she'd been accustomed to seeing in the Chamber with the Seven illuminated, its branches reaching out over the domed roof. The words that painted themselves on the ceiling were ones she'd studied a hundred times: Together we are strong and balanced.

"What does it say?" Clark asked, looking up at the brand-new words.

Liv gave him a scrutinizing look. "You can't read it?"

He shook his head.

She slipped the ring off, and the words were just ancient symbols. She realized that she was starting to understand the language. These were words she'd read many times and now understood in the founder's language.

Running the ring over the symbols, the words popped up, showing the message: Together we are strong and balanced.

"Oh, wow," Clark said. "What do you think it means?"

Liv shook her head, feeling as if she were being pushed forward. "I don't think that's what we're here to see." She pointed to the wall in front of them with the symbols glowing brightly. "I think that's it."

He agreed with a nod, and they each took a step forward.

This wall had small and large symbols, some in blue and the rest in gold. The ones in gold were divided into two columns. As before, Liv ran her ring over the first column, finding what she'd been hoping for. It was the list of the Founder families' names:

Sinclair

Beaufont

Takahashi

There were four other names she didn't recognize, which was strange. She continued to run the ring over the rest of the names.

"Why are there fourteen names?" Clark asked.

Liv scanned the ring over the words to the right of each family name. Down the first column, she found the same thing inscribed beside them all—Magicians.

Sinclair—Magician

Beaufont—Magician

Takahashi—Magician

She then ran the ring over the symbols beside the second column, but what it illuminated wasn't what she expected. Beside the other seven names was the word Mortals.

Liv spun to face Clark, her heart pounding wildly. "Oh, my God! I know what they've been hiding."

His face said that he'd seen the ring interpret the ancient language and understood. "Yes, and this is bigger than I could have even conceived."

Liv could barely speak. Her throat twice tried to close

up, and her heart jumped into her mouth. She swallowed. Took a breath. Felt her mother beside her.

"Clark, it was never the House of Seven." Liv found it hard to breathe suddenly, but finally, she inhaled raggedly. "The House was created as a partnership to balance magic. 'Together we are strong and balanced.'"

He nodded, dazed. "The House of Seven is actually the House of Fourteen, made up of both magicians and mortals."

Liv couldn't believe it, but the evidence was clearly written on the wall in the ancient language—and it made absolute sense. She looked at Clark, pure conviction in her eyes. "You know what we have to do now?"

She hadn't always understood her older brother, but right then, she knew they were aligned. He narrowed his eyes, determination strong in his gaze. "We have to find the mortals who used to be a part of this House and reinstate balance. We have to finish what Mom and Dad started."

Liv nodded. She couldn't have said it better herself.

CHAPTER THIRTY-EIGHT

I ndikos always accompanied Adler on his trips to the Black Void. It wasn't that he felt unsafe around the God Magician, but it made him feel better to have an ally if the One was in a bad mood. It hadn't been long since he had awoken him, and Adler knew the God Magician was still grouchy, although that wasn't the right term for an ancient magician who had been asleep for many, many years.

"Father," Adler called to the mostly white magician who slumped in his throne. It wasn't Adler's father, but rather his father's father's father. "How do you feel?"

The God Magician stirred, making the wind howl in Adler's ears. "I need more time. My strength is still building."

"I understand," he said in a consoling manner. "But I wanted to assure you that things are going according to plan."

He pulled the giants' sword from his back, releasing the enchantments that had kept it hidden. The full sword lit up in the dark chamber, which was full of bones and broken potion bottles. Cracks lined the wall, which mostly allowed the cold a place to come in, but they also allowed the God Magician a way out of his chamber. He'd been the one to brainwash Raina Ludwig. He'd had his hand in much lately, and it worried Adler. He wanted what his father wanted, but things were getting out of control. So many had already died, and he believed that was only the beginning. Hiding the truth had gotten exponentially more difficult.

"Set it on my lap," the God Magician said.

His skin was transparent and his long white hair was draped on the floor, curling around and around. When he opened his eyes, the two orbs of light shone brightly, nearly blinding Adler.

He shielded his face as the God Magician rested his hands on the giants' sword.

"I figured it would be safest here," Adler said, trying to blink away the burning in his eyes from the light.

A loud clattering filled the Black Void and Adler stumbled back. The sword knocked into him, the hilt hitting him across the calves, knocking him to the floor.

"That's not Turbinger," the God Magician said, his voice filling Adler's head.

"What do you mean?" Adler asked. "Of course it is."

The oldest magician in the world rose off his throne and bore down on Adler. "No, that's a fake. You've lost the real one."

"No, that's impossible. God Magician, I promise that I did everything you told me to."

"You've failed me," the first Sinclair said, his voice vibrating with ancient evil. "The truth is out there, and the girl will uncover it unless you stop her. We can't allow the prophecy to come to pass."

Adler stumbled back and straightened up. "I've got plans for her. Don't worry, she doesn't know anything. I've made sure of it."

"What of her mother's ring?"

Adler shook his head. "She died with it on."

"Are you sure?"

"Guinevere always wore her ring," Adler assured him. "And even if this is a replica, it just means the one in the Natural History Museum was the wrong one. The real one was probably destroyed long ago."

"You idiot!" the God Magician said. "Don't ruin everything. Ensure that there is no trail. It will soon be my time to rise. I will not have you lose it all for me."

Adler threw himself down, kneeling to the strongest power he'd ever known. "Do not worry, my Lord. I promise."

Before Adler was a person so powerful he'd never oppose him, but he was also fearful of what would happen when the God Magician came back into his full power.

CHAPTER THIRTY-NINE

The flowers in Liv's hands reminded her of her childhood. Lilies. They had been her mother's favorite. The sweet scent wafted up to her nose, fueled by the Santa Ana winds.

She kept her head down as she strode through the cemetery. It had been five long years since she had been here, and suddenly she felt her younger self striding beside her, as if she'd crossed into a time/space continuum where all versions of herself existed.

This is long overdue, Liv thought when she spotted the tombstone.

Liv had been avoiding finding this closure and never would have realized that it would have come like this. When she was only two feet from her parents' grave, Liv halted, the tears seeking to burst out of her.

She took a deep breath. Tightened her hands around the flowers. Felt something so deep and yearning within her. All these years she'd missed her parents badly. The pain was always there when she woke in the morning and realized they were gone. When she laid down at night and knew they wouldn't be there in the morning when she awoke. When she had a victory and realized she couldn't tell them about it. Every moment was etched by their absence. They were the best part of who she was, and yet they were gone. It didn't make any sense, but Liv now understood things so much better than she had before.

Clearing her throat, she read the words that marked their shared tombstone: Together in Life. Together in Love. Here Lie Two Souls Intertwined Forever: Warrior and Councilor.

Liv laid the flowers she'd brought on her parents' grave and backed up two feet.

"Mom. Dad," she began, interrupted by a crow cawing somewhere in the trees.

"Mom and Dad," she started again. "I'm sorry. I'm sorry I abandoned the House of… I'm sorry I abandoned our family. It's just that without you, I forgot who I was. I didn't want to be what you made me, and yet, since I've stepped back into your life, all I know how to do is what you taught me. I'm stronger than I ever was. I'm strong like you, Mommy, as if I feel your courage beating in my soul. And I hear your wisdom at every turn, Daddy."

The tears that broke free of Liv's eyes made the pain somehow more bearable. "I thought that running would make it easier, but I was wrong. Embracing my role as Warrior has brought me closer to you than I ever thought possible. Losing you will never be tolerable, but now I realize how ridiculous it was to distance myself from my family. It is only now that I feel a chance to be whole again one day."

The tears came down freely, falling down Liv's cheeks, soaking her cape, and blinding her. She fell down to her hands and knees, dropping her head, vibrating with ache.

"I love you more than anything," she cried, hardly able to breathe. "I miss you every damn day, but I know now why you risked everything."

Liv swallowed, feeling a renewed sense of hope. She lifted her chin. "I know what you died trying to uncover, and I won't let it be in vain. I will find the truth and reveal it for all. I will restore everything to what it once was. Somehow I'll take up your mission and restore balance to the House of Fourteen."

The story continues with THE LOYAL FRIEND, *coming soon. Join the email list to be notified when book five is available.*

Join the email list

Thank you to you, the reader, for reading the books and supporting the series. The other day I got a review from a reader who wanted to be Facebook friends with Liv. That was one awesome compliment. At times I like to think I'm her and you all want to be my friend, however, I'm not nearly as bad ass—at all.

Last night I woke up at my normal "witching hour" at around three o'clock in the morning. Many spiritual gurus think that this is when we're "awoken" by the universe because it's the quietest time during the day. Spirit or inspiration or whatever we want to call it is trying to send a message. Rumi, the great poet, said, "The morning breeze has secrets to tell you. Do not go back to sleep."

I listened to the poet while writing many books and actually wrote my first series, the Lucidites, between three and five o'clock in the morning. My infant would then wake up at six and I'd realize how very wrong Rumi was. But also so very right. I've had some awesome ideas during the "witching hour."

This is when you begin to wonder what the eff I'm getting to. Hold on. I'm almost there.

So I woke up today at three o'clock in the morning. This is when I usually check emails and messages, many of which I'll forget I've looked at during this ungodly hour, and then later forget to respond to them when it's a descent time of day. I need better work habits.

Anyway, this morning, I thought that inspiration had woken me up yet again when I heard a bump downstairs. The noise had woken me up. Not inspiration.

Unlike Liv Beaufont, I totally tensed. That's when I pictured the absolute worst, which is how my convoluted brain works. I imagined that the drug cartel had broken into my house because... A masked murderer had gotten so bold as to break into my house because... The hoodlums down the street were downstairs, wishing they'd broken into a house with electronics from *this* century. As the potential realities poured through my brain, the loud noises outside my bedroom continued.

I armed myself with the many weapons I keep in my bedroom. I can't tell you what those are because a Warrior never discloses her secrets. Anyway, I was about to yank back my door to assault this evil-doer, when I realized how much I wasn't like Liv Beaufont. I'm certain that when facing actual danger, I'd not swing the sword properly or thrust kick the jerk in the chest or do any of the awesome things that Liv does.

Accepting this reality, I pulled back the door to find my cat had taken a liking to the laundry basket and was thrusting his head against it, making it knock into the wall beside my bedroom.

So the good news was there was no masked murderer downstairs. The bad news was that my cat has the same affliction as me during the wee hours of the night.

I might not be Liv Beaufont, but I've got the cat who inspired Plato and although he doesn't talk, I'm pretty sure he's plotting to end my short reign of sanity.

Speaking of plotting, Michael had many of the great ideas for the end of this arc. The graveyard scene was something he was passionate about when we were discussing this book and I think it worked really well to end the arc right. Also, the last scene with Adler was something he really thought would round out the book. It's that kind of collaborating that I believe is keeping this series going strong and I hope continues for a long, long time.

MICHAEL'S AUTHOR NOTES

MARCH 25, 2019

THANK YOU for not only reading this story but these *Author Notes* as well.

(I think I've been good with always opening with "thank you." If not, I need to edit the other *Author Notes*!)

RANDOM (*sometimes*) THOUGHTS?

So, I'm reading Sarah's notes, and I get to this line:

"This is when you begin to wonder what the eff I'm getting to. Hold on.

I'm almost there."

But, the first time I read that, I read 'eff' as 'elf' and had a slight concern starting that Sarah was starting to play footsies with the unreality on the other side of her stories.

Was Sarah starting to live LIV?

Then, of course, I read she meant the word which also could mean horizontal Olympics, not the girl with pointed ears and all was right with the world.

For a moment.

It's Sarah, one should never assume the world is right around her - it's just how she rolls.

As a collaborator, what else would I want?

Sarah can claim that she is a scaredy cat (and perhaps she is) but she didn't hide UNDER the covers, she found Batman's weapons (see, totally shared your weapon stash) and then proceeded to walk over and *whack-the-shit* out of her loving and faithful cat.

I'm sure fluffy-kins would have looked up at Sarah with a 'why me?' expression as it conked over, but I digress from my point.

My point was she DID get up and go for the door.

A hero isn't someone who isn't scared. A Hero is someone who acts through their fear.

Well done, Sarah, you are a Hero!

AROUND THE WORLD IN 80 DAYS

One of the interesting (at least to me) aspects of my life is the ability to work from anywhere and at any time. In the future, I hope to re-read my own *Author Notes* and remember my life as a diary entry.

La Puente, California - about 30 minutes (on a good day) from downtown Los Angeles.

It's 7:20 AM here, and I've been out of bed about for an hour and fifteen minutes. I've spoken with Stephen Campbell (of Zen Master Walking™ fame) while he was at the airport, getting on a plane in 30 minutes for his trip back to Florida.

One of his and wife's sons pulled together a very romantic proposal and wanted to have family all around and surprise his fiancé.

(I've no idea how that went down except she said 'yes' - a good result I think.)

There are so few storms in this part of California (because there is so little rain in the last few years) that it should come as no surprise we have a significant water leak in the dining room.

I'd provide a picture, but it's kinda ugly.

Imagine that you painted a ceiling about a year ago. The paint is still pretty elastic, so when water congeals above it, it doesn't split, but rather starts creating a water-filled puss pocket on the bottom of your dining room ceiling.

Finally, with enough water, it splits the paint and all of that white water (from the gypsum board) comes down on your wood dining room set, warping it and spraying white splatters everywhere.

It looks like I have a two foot white popped pimple above me…

GROSS!

FAN PRICING

$0.99 Saturdays (new LMBPN stuff) and $0.99 Wednesday (both LMBPN books and friends of LMBPN books.) Get great stuff from us and others at tantalizing prices.

Go ahead, I bet you can't read just one.

Sign up here: http://lmbpn.com/email/.

HOW TO MARKET FOR BOOKS YOU LOVE

Review them so others have your thoughts, tell friends and the dogs of your enemies (because who wants to talk with enemies?)… *Enough said ;-)*

Ad Aeternitatem,

Michael Anderle

ACKNOWLEDGMENTS

SARAH NOFFKE

My favorite part of writing any book is creating the acknowledgements page. It reminds me that writing a book is not a solo task. I might sit alone and write, but the finished product is a result of the support and encouragement of a tribe of people.

Thank you to the readers who buy the books, read them, review and recommend. YOU are the one who keeps us writing. I'm always inspired by the messages I receive from readers. Thank you supporting the books and offering so much richness to my life.

Thank you to my LBMPN family for all the support. Steve, Michael, Lynne, Moonchild, Jennifer and so many others who help champion the book to publication and beyond.

Thank you to the beta readers who offered so many valuable insights early on. Thank you to John, Chrisa, Kelly, Martin and Larry.

Thank you to the JIT team for all the awesome feedback. A new series is always exciting and nerve-wracking.

Michael and I thought we had a great idea for a new world, but we don't really know until we get objective feedback. What would I do without all you awesome readers?

Thank you to my friends and family. Writing is a strange profession. I work weird hours, talk to myself, have a strange diet, get antsy about deadlines. But the wonderful people in my life continue to show their encouragement and thoughtfulness no matter what. It is never lost on me because I know that I wouldn't be doing what I love without all you amazing people, cheering me on.

And as with all my books, the final thank you goes to my muse, Lydia. I wrote my first book so that I could make my daughter proud, and it's never stopped. I write every book for you, my love.

BOOKS BY SARAH NOFFKE

Sarah Noffke, an Amazon Best Seller, writes YA and NA sci-fi fantasy, paranormal and urban fantasy. She is the author of the Lucidites, Reverians, Ren, Vagabond Circus, Olento Research, Soul Stone Mage, Ghost Squadron and Precious Galaxy series. Noffke holds a Masters of Management and teaches college business courses. Most of her students have no idea that she toils away her hours crafting fictional characters. Noffke's books are top rated and best-sellers on Kindle. Currently, she has thirty-three novels published. Her books are available in paperback, audio and in Spanish, Portuguese and Italian. http://www.sarahnoffke.com

Check out other work by this author here.

Ghost Squadron:

Formation #1:

Kill the bad guys. Save the Galaxy. All in a hard day's work.

After ten years of wandering the outer rim of the galaxy, Eddie Teach is a man without a purpose. He was one of the toughest pilots in the Federation, but now he's just a regular guy, getting into bar fights and making a difference wherever he can. It's not the same as flying a ship and saving colonies, but it'll have to do.

That is, until General Lance Reynolds tracks Eddie down and offers him a job. There are bad people out there, plotting terrible things, killing innocent people, and destroying entire colonies. **Someone has to stop them.**

Eddie, along with the genetically-enhanced combat pilot Julianna Fregin and her trusty E.I. named Pip, must recruit a diverse team of specialists, both human and alien. They'll need to master their new Q-Ship, one of the most powerful strike ships ever constructed. And finally, they'll have to stop a faceless enemy so powerful, it threatens to destroy the entire Federation.

All in a day's work, right?

Experience this exciting military sci-fi saga and the latest addition to the expanded Kurtherian Gambit Universe. If you're a fan of Mass Effect, Firefly, or Star Wars, you'll love this riveting new space opera.

NOTE: If cursing is a problem, then this might not be for you.

Check out the entire series <u>here</u>.

The Precious Galaxy Series:

Corruption #1

A new evil lurks in the darkness.

After an explosion, the crew of a battlecruiser mysteriously disappears.

Bailey and Lewis, complete strangers, find themselves suddenly onboard the damaged ship. Lewis hasn't worked a case in years, not since the final one broke his spirit and his bank account. The last thing Bailey remembers is preparing to take down a fugitive on Onyx Station.

Mysteries are harder to solve when there's no evidence left behind.

Bailey and Lewis don't know how they got onboard *Ricky Bobby* or why. However, they quickly learn that whatever was responsible for the explosion and disappearance of the crew is still on the ship.

Monsters are real and what this one can do changes everything.

The new team bands together to discover what happened and how to fight the monster lurking in the bottom of the battlecruiser.

Will they find the missing crew? Or will the monster end them all?

The Soul Stone Mage Series:

House of Enchanted #1:

The Kingdom of Virgo has lived in peace for thousands of years...until now.

The humans from Terran have always been real assholes to the witches of Virgo. Now a silent war is brewing, and the timing couldn't be worse. Princess Azure will soon be crowned queen of the Kingdom of Virgo.

In the Dark Forest a powerful potion-maker has been murdered.

Charmsgood was the only wizard who could stop a deadly virus plaguing Virgo. He also knew about the devastation the people from Terran had done to the forest.

Azure must protect her people. Mend the Dark Forest. Create alliances with savage beasts. No biggie, right?

But on coronation day everything changes. Princess Azure isn't who she thought she was and that's a big freaking problem.

Welcome to The Revelations of Oriceran. Check out the entire series here.

The Lucidites Series:

Awoken, #1:

Around the world humans are hallucinating after sleepless nights.

In a sterile, underground institute the forecasters keep reporting the same events.

And in the backwoods of Texas, a sixteen-year-old girl is about to be caught up in a fierce, ethereal battle.

Meet Roya Stark. She drowns every night in her dreams, spends her hours reading classic literature to avoid her family's ridicule, and is prone to premonitions—which are becoming more frequent. And now her dreams are filled with strangers offering to reveal what she has always wanted to know: Who is she? That's the question that haunts her, and she's about to find out. But will Roya live to regret learning the truth?

Stunned, #2

Revived, #3

The Reverians Series:

Defects, #1:

In the happy, clean community of Austin Valley, everything appears to be perfect. Seventeen-year-old Em Fuller, however, fears something is askew. Em is one of the new generation of Dream Travelers. For some reason, the gods have not seen fit to gift all of them with their expected special abilities. Em is a Defect—one of the unfortunate Dream Travelers not gifted with a psychic power. Desperate to do whatever it takes to earn her gift, she endures painful daily injections along with commands from her overbearing, loveless father. One of the few bright spots in her life is the return of a friend she had thought dead—but with his return comes the knowledge of a shocking, unforgivable truth. The society Em thought was protecting her has actually been betraying her, but she has no idea how to break away from its authority without hurting everyone she loves.

Rebels, #2
Warriors, #3

Vagabond Circus Series:

Suspended, #1:

When a stranger joins the cast of Vagabond Circus—a circus that is run by Dream Travelers and features real magic—mysterious events start happening. The once orderly grounds of the circus become riddled with hidden threats. And the ringmaster realizes not only are his circus and its magic at risk, but also his very life.

Vagabond Circus caters to the skeptics. Without skeptics, it would close its doors. This is because Vagabond Circus runs for two reasons and only two reasons: first and foremost to provide the lost and lonely Dream Travelers a place to be illustrious. And secondly, to show the nonbelievers that there's still magic in the world. If they believe, then they care, and if they care, then they don't destroy. They stop the small abuse that day-by-day breaks down humanity's spirit. If Vagabond Circus makes one skeptic believe in magic, then they halt the cycle, just a little bit. They allow a little more love into this world. That's Dr. Dave Raydon's mission. And that's why this ringmaster recruits. That's why he directs. That's why he puts on a show that makes people question their beliefs. He wants the world to believe in magic once again.

Paralyzed, #2

Released, #3

Ren Series:

Ren: The Man Behind the Monster, #1:

Born with the power to control minds, hypnotize others, and read thoughts, Ren Lewis, is certain of one thing: God made a mistake. No one should be born with so much power. A monster awoke in him the same year he received his gifts. At ten years old. A prepubescent boy with the ability to control others might merely abuse his powers, but Ren allowed it to corrupt him. And since he can have and do anything he wants, Ren should be happy.

However, his journey teaches him that harboring so much power doesn't bring happiness, it steals it. Once this realization sets in, Ren makes up his mind to do the one thing that can bring his tortured soul some peace. He must kill the monster.

Note This book is NA and has strong language, violence and sexual references.

Ren: God's Little Monster, #2
Ren: The Monster Inside the Monster, #3
Ren: The Monster's Adventure, #3.5
Ren: The Monster's Death

Olento Research Series:

Alpha Wolf, #1:
Twelve men went missing.

Six months later they awake from drug-induced stupors to find themselves locked in a lab.

And on the night of a new moon, eleven of those men, possessed by new—and inhuman—powers, break out of their prison and race through the streets of Los Angeles until they disappear one by one into the night.

Olento Research wants its experiments back. Its CEO, Mika Lenna, will tear every city apart until he has his werewolves imprisoned once again. He didn't undertake a huge risk just to lose his would-be assassins.

However, the Lucidite Institute's main mission is to save the world from injustices. Now, it's Adelaide's job to find these mutated men and protect them and society, and fast. Already around the nation, wolflike men are being spotted. Attacks on innocent women are happening. And then, Adelaide realizes what her next step must be: She has to find the alpha wolf first. Only once she's located him can she stop whoever is behind this experiment to create wild beasts out of human beings.

BOOKS BY MICHAEL ANDERLE

For a complete list of books by Michael Anderle, please visit:

www.lmbpn.com/ma-books/

All LMBPN Audiobooks are Available at Audible.com and iTunes

To see all LMBPN audiobooks, including those written by
Michael Anderle please visit:

www.lmbpn.com/audible

CONNECT WITH THE AUTHORS

Connect with Sarah and sign up for her email list here:

http://www.sarahnoffke.com/connect/

You can catch her podcast, LA Chicks, here:

http://lachicks.libsyn.com/

Connect with Michael Anderle and sign up for his email list here:

Website: http://lmbpn.com

Email List: http://lmbpn.com/email/

Facebook:
www.facebook.com/TheKurtherianGambitBooks